Maria Grace pai
emotion – Cindy H.

Praise ...*with Grace*

"Grace has quickly become one of my favorite authors of Austen-inspired fiction. Her love of Austen's characters and the Regency era shine through in all of her novels." **Diary of an Eccentric**

"Maria Grace is stunning and emotional, and readers will be blown away by the uniqueness of her plot and characterization" **Savvy Wit and Verse**

"Maria Grace has once again brought to her readers a delightful, entertaining and sweetly romantic story while using Austen's characters as a launching point for the tale." **Calico Critic**

I believe that this is what Maria Grace does best, blend old and new together to create a story that has the framework of Austen and her characters, but contains enough new and exciting content to keep me turning the pages. ... Grace's style is not to be missed.. **From the desk of Kimberly Denny-Ryder**

Snowbound at Hartfield

Maria Grace

White Soup Press

Published by: White Soup Press

Snowbound at Hartfield
Copyright © January 2017 Maria Grace

For information, address
author.MariaGrace@gmail.com

ISBN-10: 0-9980937-2-6
ISBN-13: 978-0-9980937-2-7 (White Soup Press)

Author's Website: RandomBitsofFaascination.com
Email address: Author.MariaGrace@gmail.com

Dedication

For my husband and sons.
You have always believed in me.

Chapter 1

I do not want people to be agreeable, as it saves me the trouble of liking them a great deal. — Jane Austen

COLONEL RICHARD FITZWILLIAM pulled the scarf a little tighter around his neck. If the winds grew any stronger, they might topple the coach.

What madness had seized the weather? Snow was unusual enough, but a storm such as this? Who would have expected it? Certainly not his cousin Darcy. Careful and meticulous as he was, he would never have set out if he had any inkling a blizzard were a possibility, especially in the company of his wife and father-in-law.

The Darcy carriage was as snug and warm as such a vehicle might be in such anomalous weather. For that he could be glad. They were not in imminent danger of freezing to death. Still, the winds howled just as the wind on the French plains before—

No! He clenched his gloved hands into fists. Returning there, even in memory alone, did him no favors. Elizabeth—Liza as she permitted him to call her now, mostly to annoy Darcy—Liza reminded him to remember the past only as it gave him pleasure. She was right. He must do precisely that.

He drew a deep breath, then another, forcing his clenched hands to open. *Warm fires, fine port, good company.* His heart slowed just a bit.

She was watching him from the corner of her eye. She knew. She always knew.

Perhaps they would talk about it later. But first, they needed shelter.

The first inn they had stopped at had no room available at any price. Now, Darcy was inquiring at a decidedly seedy-looking establishment, the Ram's Horn. Seedy was better than no shelter at all, though it meant there would be little sleep to be had for any of them. Still, he would count it good fortune if Darcy's blunt could smooth the way to a room and a warm fire for the night.

The coach door creaked open. A blast of wind and snow burst in ahead of Darcy who jumped in and slammed the door behind him.

"Were you able to procure rooms?" Fitzwilliam pulled his coat tighter around his chest, shoulder throbbing with the fresh burst of freezing air.

"No. Not even the baronet who arrived just after we did could command lodgings."

Liza gasped and glanced at her father who hunched for warmth and rubbed his hands together.

Darcy lifted his hand with a mildly dramatic flair.

How Liza had changed him.

"That is not to say we do not have accommodations though. The hand of Providence has provided in a most unexpected way. Just inside the inn, I encountered an old school friend of mine, George Knightley, who lives but a mile from here. He has invited us—and the baronet and his daughter—to stay with him."

"What a spot of good luck." Bennet nodded vigorously, perhaps to cover his shivering.

It seemed far too easy that Darcy's old school chum just happened to be there, only too ready to extend an offer of hospitality. Nothing in life ever proved so convenient. Fate would surely exact some sort of price for this succor.

Still, refusing would be foolish.

Darcy finished telling them about his acquaintance with Knightley just as the coach pulled up to Hartfield's front steps, the baronet's coach just behind. No doubt, Darcy's characteristic brevity managed to leave out the most interesting parts.

By his description, Knightley seemed decidedly odd. Why did a married man, with an estate as respectable as Donwell Abbey, live at his father-in-law's neighboring establishment? It was just not done.

Darcy's friends were usually so conventional.

Then again, Bennet proved decidedly odd himself. Darcy had learned to tolerate him with greater equanimity over the—what was it now, fifteen months?—of his marriage to Liza.

Perhaps Darcy was becoming less particular about his connections.

He handed Liza out of the carriage and steadied

Bennet as he followed.

Fitzwilliam stepped into the wind and skidded on a patch of ice, barely catching himself on the carriage door.

Blast and botheration! This was not fit weather for man nor beast.

Sir Walter Elliot climbed into the coach, leaving the door open until the driver closed it. There had been little enough warm air within as it was. It would have been nice for him to try to preserve it. But the act of closing the door himself might have been enough to compromise his dignity. He could not have that, could he?

Elizabeth Elliot pulled her hood over her head and huddled into it. The fur within was cold, too. Yes, it would warm soon, but her teeth chattered in the meantime, and Father would likely scold her for the noise.

Thoughtless, self-absorbed ...

No, those thoughts were ungracious and unsuitable, and Lady Russell would probably scold her for it. She scolded over so many matters, so what was one more added to the list? Elizabeth bit her lip and pulled the edges of her hood around her face.

Another unkind thought.

Surely it was this horrid storm that had compromised her composure. Usually she was better than this.

She had to be. There was little choice. Father was so very particular about all things that touched his pride—vanity, really. It was not worth the consequences if she vexed him.

Father brushed the snow off his shoulders and stomped his feet. The carriage lurched into motion.

"There was no room at the inn?"

"There was not." He smoothed his coat over his lap. "But being a baronet has its privileges. I have made arrangements."

"What kind of arrangements?" She cringed. Father's arrangements usually did not consider their budget and cost them in privation later—not that he would ever admit to it, but they did. And it would inevitably fall to her to make some way to provide for his comfort despite whatever he had done.

She had become quite good at it.

"The inn was dreadful, totally unsuitable." He waved his gloved hand dismissively. "But there I met the leading gentleman of this little community. He recognized the honor of hosting a family of our rank and invited us to stay at his estate."

"Do you know this man?" She covered her face with her hand.

There had been many so-called gentlemen that had proved themselves otherwise. Pray there would be a lock on her door tonight. Even if there was, it might be best that her maid sleep with her as well.

"I do not. But he introduced me to his friend Darcy, whom he also invited to stay, and though that family does not have a title, they are connected to Matlock, and that is recommendation enough for me." Father settled back in that attitude that declared the conversation over.

Of course connections would be enough for him.

Stop now. That thought was headed nowhere productive—or polite.

She sucked in a long slow breath, and another. The

searing cold air made her head ache, but it slowed her thoughts enough to rein them in.

The Darcy reputation was well known, and it was impeccable. Even his surprise marriage to a country gentleman's daughter had not tarnished it. What was more, his wife was very well received herself. A credit to the Darcy name, she had been called. Perhaps the friend of such a family would be more gentlemanly than not.

The coach rolled to a stop.

She would find out soon enough.

Fitzwilliam stomped snow from his boots as he ascended the front stairs. Knightley himself opened the door for them. "Pray come in."

Warmth and light the color of a roaring fire poured through the door. No matter how peculiar the man might be, the invitation was too inviting to ignore.

Mother would approve of the vestibule—tasteful, neat, and a bit old fashioned. She always maintained that traditional décor spoke of taste and respect when it was clean and well preserved. The house seemed all those things.

But most of all it was warm. Delightfully, soothingly warm.

Fitzwilliam unwrapped his scarf.

A startled-looking butler met them and took their coats.

A woman, who must have been the housekeeper, trundled up to Knightley.

"Prepare rooms for our guests and their servants. Send the grooms for their horses." Knightley ducked around the housekeeper. "Emma! Emma!"

Darcy cringed.

No surprise. One did not bellow for his wife as one did a servant.

Bennet sniggered under his breath.

There was a reason the younger Bennet girls were not known for their fine manners. But best not dwell upon that now.

Liza smiled softly, slipped her arm in Darcy's, and pressed her shoulder to his. His tension eased. She was a master at restoring his composure.

Lucky man.

Thankfully, Darcy seemed to appreciate that fact and treated his wife very well. Anything less would have made him intolerable.

A young woman, blonde and pretty-ish, and looking not much older than Georgiana, hurried down the grand stairs. "I was so worried with you out there in the weather!"

Knightley caught her hands in his. "Now you are sounding like your dear papa. As you see, I am quite well and have brought guests seeking shelter from the storm. May I present Sir Walter and Miss Elliot of Kellynch Hall?"

No wonder they looked so familiar!

And offended.

Clearly Sir Walter did not appreciate being presented to the mistress of the house when he clearly outranked her. The question was, did Knightley do it intentionally or were his manners that sloppy?

Interesting.

"I am pleased to make your acquaintance." Mrs. Knightley curtsied with girlish energy, far better suited to a miss than a missus.

"I am most pleased to renew our acquaintance, sir." Fitzwilliam stepped forward and bowed.

Sir Walter looked at him, forehead knotted and brows drawn together.

"Colonel Fitzwilliam?" Miss Elliot peered at him, eyes widening. "Father, you recall, we were introduced by the Dalrymples, at a card party, three, or was it four months ago?"

"Fitzwilliam? Oh, you are Earl Matlock's son!"

Amazing how the man's countenance brightened at that memory.

Fitzwilliam bowed. "Yes sir, I am. This is my cousin, Mr. Darcy, Mrs. Darcy, and her father, Mr. Bennet."

Sir Walter bowed from his shoulders, just enough to be proper. Miss Elliot's curtsey demonstrated a touch more civility. Just as they had at Bath.

Their haughtiness had not won them many friends there. In truth, though, it was more the baronet, than his daughter whom people avoided. When she was apart from her father, uncommon as it was, she seemed rather pleasant.

The tall, dark-haired woman might have once been regarded handsome, but years on the shelf left her worn and weary along the edges. A little like her garments—once fashionable, but now a bit threadbare. Society was not kind to women who did not 'take' soon enough.

Knightley took his wife's hand as she descended the last few steps.

Given his expression, he was as fond of his wife as Darcy was of Liza. Perhaps that was the common disposition he and Darcy shared.

Knightley tucked his wife's hand into the crook of

his arm. "Darcy is an old school chum of mine. Imagine encountering him in Highbury at such a time."

"That is very good luck, indeed. You are all very welcome. I should very much like to hear tales of my husband's school days. He rarely mentions them." Mrs. Knightley's eyes twinkled with a hint of mischief, much like Liza's did.

Knightley flashed his brows at Darcy.

What was that?

Darcy never indulged in any sort of high spiritedness during his school days, did he? The look on Knightley's face suggested otherwise. That was one conversation Fitzwilliam would definitely follow up on.

This could be a very interesting house party after all.

"Oh, Papa!" Mrs. Knightley hurried past them.

An elderly man, wrapped in a warm banyan, scarf and soft cap, shuffled toward them. "What … what is this commotion? Such disruptions are not good for the digestion."

Mrs. Knightley wrapped her arm in his, supporting him. "Knightley has brought us guests, Papa."

"Guests, in a snowstorm? It is a most dangerous thing to be out in such weather. I do not see why anyone with sense would be out on such a day. I still do not understand why Knightley had to go into town."

She patted his hand. "That is why he invited them to stay with us. They were caught by the storm whilst traveling."

"I see, I see. Traveling is a trial indeed. No one should be out in this weather." He nodded somberly. He blinked several times, and his eyes widened. "But are there children with them? They bear disease you know—"

"No, there are no children. Why do we not go to the parlor, and you may become acquainted with them. I will send for tea." Mrs. Knightley guided him down the corridor, muttering under his breath as he walked.

That was the reason Knightley lived at Hartfield, not Donwell Abbey—to care for the old man in his dotage. Sounded like exactly the kind of man Darcy would befriend.

Knightley urged them toward the parlor.

Elizabeth Elliot snuck a glance at her father. His forehead was creased, and his lips pressed into a very distinct expression that only meant one thing: disgust. Proximity to the old and infirm brought it out. He no longer bothered to hide it.

He used to, before they took residence in Bath. But there he encountered so many 'unfortunates' that the expression took up long-term residence, much as they had.

Was Mr. Knightley merely ignoring it, or could it really have escaped his attention?

Best to assume the former. His hospitality was too generous to risk offending him. The question was how to avoid it now that Father had begun along that path? If only she knew him well enough—or at all really—to be able to appeal to his vanity or ego. Perhaps a few compliments to his wife. Considering the looks he gave her, that might be his weakness.

The girl looked barely old enough to be married. Did she understand her good fortune, to have a husband at all, much less one who looked at her as

Knightley did? As Wentworth did Anne?

Oh, that sounded far too close to jealousy for comfort. Best focus on something else.

Mrs. Darcy. She did not seem a typical society matron—no, that line of thinking would not end well either. Mr. Darcy gazed at her the way Knightley did at his wife.

Colonel Fitzwilliam.

He was a well-looking man. A bit weather-beaten to be sure. If not guided away from it, Father would remark upon that. He did so freely enough in Bath.

But tours of duty on the continent did that to a man. It was only to be expected.

She had heard from those who knew Fitzwilliam that he had seen battle against Napoleon. Few, if any, of the officers she knew could claim that. Colonel Fitzwilliam never spoke of it, though. He never spoke of his service at all.

It made one curious.

Still, he was the son of an earl, and his manners showed it. Refined and polished, every time they met. Perhaps he might prove agreeable company for the duration of their visit if she was not confined to the company of the two resident matrons.

There was little worse than to be in the exclusive company of married women when one was unmarried. Always so full of advice about how to catch a husband.

As if she had not heard it all already.

Dreadful, truly dreadful. A shiver coursed down her spine, and she pulled her shawl a little tighter.

If it became too uncomfortable, she could always claim a headache and keep to her rooms. No one would be surprised if any of their number took colds from being out in the weather. Perhaps it would be a good idea to simply avoid the inevitable now and ask to be excused.

Mrs. Knightley beckoned them into the parlor. Her smile held such warmth and enthusiasm—it would be most ungrateful to try to withdraw now. Surely this company could not be any worse than what she had experienced in Bath—and none of them had ever offered her a warm fire and shelter against a storm. Such generous and ready hospitality deserved equal efforts on her part.

Fitzwilliam rubbed his aching hands together. A blazing fire crackled in the fireplace of the old-style parlor. With heavy drapes drawn against the chill outside and pillows and blankets heaped upon the furniture, the chamber could hardly be more snug. Under other circumstances, the room would have been far too hot, but until the cold left his bones, it was entirely and perfectly warm.

Mrs. Knightley seated her father in a large leather chair very near the fire and tucked a lap blanket across his knees. He leaned back and briefly closed his eyes, as though completely content with the world. She kissed his cheek.

What a fortunate man to have someone so devoted to his comfort. His sisters would have sent a servant to tend Father.

"Pray, be comfortable. I shall see to tea and your rooms." Mrs. Knightley curtsied and hurried out.

Fitzwilliam edged back to let the others seat themselves. People always revealed themselves in such moments. In such unfamiliar surroundings, information was … comforting.

No, he was not facing battle. He was not even in hostile territory, but still, whatever would calm the edgy restlessness foreign environs aroused was worth seeking.

Darcy sat beside Liza on a plump settee just far enough from the fireplace to be comfortably warm, leaving the closer seating for Bennet and Sir Walter who both seemed particularly susceptible to the cold. Not that the baronet would ever admit to feeling something so common as cold. That would be far too base for him to acknowledge.

Miss Elliot hovered near a wall. Was she hesitant in choosing a seat? The distance she kept between herself and her father suggested that she did not wish to be too near him, probably enough of that in the carriage. But she vacillated between the sofa and a single prim, feminine chair, as though she did not know whether or not to sit too close to anyone else.

His sister Rosalind did that often enough when she was not certain of the quality of the company and unwilling to encourage closer contact with someone who might not be of suitable status.

The expression Miss Elliot wore was not nearly as confident as Rosalind's, though. More like Darcy's when confronted with unfamiliar society.

Interesting.

Fitzwilliam had encountered the Elliots regularly in Bath, keeping much of the same society. Miss Elliot was a fair card player, though she did not play for more than pennies—wise considering her father's circumstances. On the dance floor she was graceful and skilled. Given her propensity to attend the same concerts as he, her taste in music seemed very like his. Why had they not spoken more?

He sat on the sofa and caught her eye, gesturing subtly next to himself. She dipped her head almost imperceptibly and sat beside him, the corner of her lips lifting just a mite. She did not look at him, though. But why would she? Propriety would declare it far too bold an act.

Knightley pulled a chair closer to his father-in-law and sat, elbows braced on his knees. "Pray forgive me if it is too familiar a question, Darcy, but how did you come to be traveling in this most disagreeable weather?"

Darcy shifted slightly in his seat as though that would make the words come more easily. He was not talkative at the best of times, and now, after the strain of traveling under such dangerous conditions, conversation would be positively vexing for him.

Fitzwilliam cleared his throat loudly enough to bring all eyes to fix on him. "I fear I am to blame for our journey. I have just received news of the death of my mother's cousin. Unbeknownst to me, he made me his heir. It would appear I am now the master of a modest estate not far from here. Darcy and Bennet have graciously consented to view the property with me and offer their opinions."

Darcy coughed, and Liza pressed her foot to the top of his. Her feet were so tiny compared to his. No doubt she was warning him not to mention that Bennet was there to learn as much as Fitzwilliam himself.

Their covert communications were jolly good fun to pick out. It would probably make Darcy quite mad to know that he did it—which only made it better sport. Did Knightley and his wife communicate that way as well? It might be worth watching them, too.

"Do you by chance speak of Listingbrook?" Knightley laced his hands together and sat up a little straighter.

The expression on his face was a very good sign.

"Do you know it?"

"I do indeed. A very pretty place. Markham's death came as a real surprise. He seemed hale and hearty at dinner with the Westons just the week before. The whole parish has been at sixes and sevens waiting for the new master to arrive."

"So the estate was well-managed?" Darcy leaned forward, eyes fixed on Knightley.

Of course, land management would draw him into the conversation.

Miss Elliot's attention pricked up as well. Odd, why would she be interested?

"Well-managed and innovative. He was forever searching out the latest information in farming and applying it to his land. Spent many an hour in my study discussing his ideas. Mind you, not all his farmers appreciated his interference, but those who did not fight him tooth and nail have shown strong returns. They credit him for it, and the hold-outs were beginning to take notice. He will be missed for certain at spring planting."

Darcy glanced at Fitzwilliam with raised eyebrows.

Did he have to gloat?

"That is very promising indeed." Darcy steepled his hands and tapped them against his chin.

Bennet snorted. "Save your lecture, Darcy. Now is not the time. I have been studying everything you have sent me, though I remain unconvinced." He turned toward Mr. Woodhouse and Sir Walter. "What think you gentlemen of the new farming methods these young men are trying to foist upon us?"

Sir Walter's nose wrinkled. "I leave such matters in the hands of my steward, though I am suspicious of these 'scientific' methods. It is his business to understand such things."

"Are you pleased with your harvests?" Knightley leaned back and cocked his head.

Sir Walter looked baffled, and a not a little affronted.

Miss Elliot's gaze dropped to her lap, and she covered her mouth with her hand.

"I have no particular farmland to be concerned with. All the farm land here is in Knightley's hands. From what I hear, he manages it very well. His friend farmer Martin seeks his advice regularly." Woodhouse worried the edge of the blanket with thumb and forefinger. "But is this not an unusual conversation for mixed company? I cannot image the ladies to be very pleased with it."

"Of course you are correct, Mr. Woodhouse." Liza smiled at the old man exactly as Mrs. Knightley had. "What do you wish to discuss?"

Mrs. Knightley flashed her an appreciative smile. How did Liza always seem to know the right thing to do and say?

Woodhouse blinked. "I … I do not know. I usually leave such things to Emma. She is so good at making people feel comfortable." He glanced over his shoulder, looking a little lost, painfully forlorn.

Prickly, itchy silence expanded in the room.

"Do you enjoy the theater, Mr. Knightley?" Miss Elliot glanced at Fitzwilliam.

She had very fine eyes.

"I confess we are home bodies, much like the Darcys, I expect, unless Darcy has changed dramatically from our school days. We rarely go into town or even much beyond Highbury. There are occasionally concerts or productions at our local assembly rooms. Our friends the Coles enjoy home theatricals and often invite us to watch."

Fitzwilliam bit his tongue. Home theatricals? They might be all the rage, but Mother deemed them positively boorish. Not that her opinion held much sway with his siblings. Darcy, though, would no sooner perform to strangers in his home than he would in a public place.

Sir Walter looked as though he shared similar opinions.

Miss Elliot wrung her hands in her lap. "We enjoyed the most brilliant concert in Bath just last month."

"Was it by chance the trio from Italy?" Fitzwilliam caught her gaze briefly.

The creases beside her eyes eased a bit. "Indeed it was. I do not recall seeing you that evening. Were you there?"

"We were a bit late arriving and sat at the back. I saw you and your father at the front of the room."

Sir Walter sat up a little straighter. "Ah yes, I remember, we attended with our cousins, the Dowager Viscountess Dalrymple, and her daughter, the Honorable Miss Carteret."

"Were those the ladies I saw you escorting at the Pump Room?"

"Indeed they were." Sir Walter thumbed his lapels. "A fine place to take the waters, the Pump Room."

"And to be seen, I suppose." Fitzwilliam shrugged.

Sir Walter's eyes narrowed, and his look turned dark.

Liza glared at him with a similar expression. Must she do that? She looked just like Mother when she did that.

"I do believe I have seen you in the Pump Room, in the company of your sisters, I assume." Sir Walter harrumphed under his breath.

"Quite true. What use is a younger brother, but as an escort of last resort? I do tire of that sport, though, parading about like game birds of sorts."

Sir Walter's eyes bulged.

Oh, this was far too easy! Liza did not approve of him indulging in such low-hanging amusements. But truly, the pompous man deserved it.

Miss Elliot's brows drew together, and the corners of her mouth drooped. "It can be an exhausting show."

"How can you say that?" Sir Walter's chest puffed a bit. "What is more significant than being seen in the right company, by the right company?"

Fitzwilliam rolled his eyes. Father was apt to intimate the same sentiments.

Did Miss Elliot just roll her eyes, too? "Of course, Father."

Liza pressed her lips together and snuck a glance at Bennet.

Bennet's lips twitched with his efforts to be somber, but clearly he was enjoying himself far too much. "All that preening and parading is very well, I suppose, when one has unmarried daughters to match off to young dandies equally fond of the parade, eh Lizzy?"

"Papa, do not tease so, I pray you. You must forgive him. My last sister is lately married. We have just finished celebrating her wedding."

"You mean your youngest sister?" Sir Walter asked.

"No, sir, my youngest sister was the first among us to marry." Liza glanced narrowly at her father.

It was still difficult for Darcy to reconcile being related to Wickham. That he was as gracious to Bennet as he was revealed the depth of his character. Not one in ten men could boast of the forbearance Darcy possessed.

"Mine was, too," Miss Elliot muttered with a similar stare at Sir Walter.

Sir Walter grunted and looked away.

Interesting, very interesting.

"I am entirely finished with all manner of match-making and courtship and shall be happy now to keep to my bookroom, my job as a father done." Bennet brushed his palms together and folded his arms over his chest.

"It was a sad day when my Isabella married and moved away with John Knightley. But my Emma did not leave me when she married." Mr. Woodhouse's rheumy eyes shimmered.

Pray let him not begin to weep!

"Of course I did not, Papa." Mrs. Knightley ushered in the maid bearing the tea service. "How could I ever leave you?" She kissed his cheek.

The maid arranged the tea service on the low table.

"Your rooms will be ready after tea. It seems, though, I have missed some interesting conversation. Pray do not let me interrupt."

"You were about to tell us your opinions on the Italian trio we heard in Bath, Colonel." Miss Elliot looked directly at him, her eyes a mixture of politeness and pleading.

"Ah, yes…"

Funny how a little storytelling allowed him to portion off part of his consciousness to observe his audience. The Darcys and Knightleys listened with polite interest. Bennet watched Sir Walter, probably looking for more fuel for his acerbic wit. Woodhouse seemed to be nodding off.

Miss Elliot, though, she regarded him with rapt attention, as though truly interested in what he had to say. Better still, she offered questions and her own opinions, which pleasingly differed just enough from his to provide for a lively discussion.

What a surprisingly diverting conversation.

A gust of wind rattled the windows. Perhaps, if he were fortunate, this storm would last several days, days that might be spent in further agreeable conversation, and getting to know a very intriguing baronet's daughter.

Chapter 2

Elizabeth Elliot's maid secured a final curl with a pin and tucked a bit of ribbon into her coiffure. "Is this what you wanted, Miss?"

The affected French accent was annoying, but it allowed both of them to maintain the illusion that she could afford a French maid.

Elizabeth examined her profile in the mirror and patted her hair. "Yes, yes, that is very good."

"Will there be anything else, madam? Your wool shawl perhaps?" She tucked the shawl around Elizabeth's shoulders.

"Yes, that will do nicely. You may go now." She rose and stepped back until she could see her entire reflection.

Her posture was still perfect, as elegant and columnar as a fashion plate. Her gown was several seasons from being the height of fashion, but the current company did not seem the type to take notice of that fact, especially if she wore it well.

Winds raged outside, but the guest room was warm and snug. Yes, it was furnished rather plainly, but plain and well-maintained had become increasingly appealing.

How Anne would laugh if she knew.

She turned this way and that. Her skirt swished, the candlelight glinting off the deep blue fabric. It looked very well in the evening light. Was it foolish to look forward to the company this evening? A dinner without pretense, without concern for being in the right company, without the sense of performing for an unknown audience—when was the last time that had happened?

All their social engagements in Bath had been about making connections, being seen with connections, being good connections. Never about being good company or enjoying good company. That concern evaporated with William Elliot's defection to Penelope.

After all this time, one would think his name would not still raise a pang in her heart. But one would be wrong.

Lady Russell had been correct. Anne should have been enough company for her.

But Anne was dull; she did not care for company, and she was ever going on about budgets and economy. Penelope enjoyed shopping and parties and always agreed with her. Of course she would choose her friend over her sister.

What a mistake.

Had Anne been there in Bath from the beginning,

Mr. Elliot would never have met Penelope. Even if he had formed an attachment to Anne, it would have ended in their marriage. Anne would never have been set up as a mistress. While it would have been her younger sister established as mistress of Kellynch, eyebrows would be raised, but it all would have been respectable and without scandal.

She sat on the edge of the bed and dabbed her eyes with her handkerchief.

It all could have been prevented.

She knew better now. Would her vow to listen to advice, even unpleasant advice, make any difference? Would Providence approve her pledge to value mundane qualities like honesty, constancy, and activity matter at all? If only she could prove her earnestness. Surely that would count in her favor, would it not?

These new acquaintances offered the perfect opportunity. They did not know her. She could be the new woman she believed herself to be—one Anne and Lady Russell might approve of—at least a little.

But Father could ruin it all with his … pompous attitudes.

There, she had said the word.

Pompous. Pretentious. Arrogant. Haughty.

Yes, he was titled and in possession—after a fashion—of a lovely country seat. That entitled him to a certain amount of pride, but since they had been forced to leave Kellynch and retrench, his pride had transformed into something more. Something dark and poisonous that tainted every social engagement and even threatened to turn him against her. If something did not change soon, they might well find themselves entirely unwelcome in good company. Worse, he could decide she was no longer a social asset and no longer welcome in his home.

Then what?

All the more reason not to waste the opportunity before her.

She checked the mirror one more time and left.

"Brush the coat again." Fitzwilliam pulled off the garment and handed it back to his valet.

"As you say, sir." Which was to say he thought it utterly unnecessary, but knew better than to speak it aloud.

That was good enough.

He checked his cravat in the mirror, unchanged from its state moments ago. Just a bit of a tug to straighten the crease. Not quite as perfect as the baronet's, but it would do.

Sir Walter's cravat might have been sketched for a valet's guidebook. Perhaps the baronet's man could give his own a few pointers.

"Your coat, sir."

He shrugged the coat over his shoulders and fastened the buttons while staring in the mirror. He turned to the side and examined his profile. Still a passable figure. Not the young man who had left for the army years ago but still respectable. Not fit for a dandy, but that was hardly a desirable image, either.

It was enough.

It was all he had.

With a final tug to his sleeves, he left.

Liza peered out of the hall window, Darcy standing—no, hovering—behind her. Besotted, utterly besotted.

Since his marriage, he rarely permitted much distance between them and did not appreciate it when it was enforced. Mother had made that mistake—once.

Fitzwilliam would have lost his meager fortune betting that Darcy would never be so taken by a woman. Apparently impossible things did happen, at least on occasion.

Winds howled on the other side of the glass, blowing away the tidy mounds of snow that had gathered on the mullions.

"I do not recall ever seeing snowfall like this." Liza turned away from the window and tucked the curtain back into place. "I fear the storm is growing worse."

"I expect we may have to impose upon Hartfield's hospitality another day at least. I would certainly not permit guests to travel under such conditions and cannot imagine Knightley doing differently." Darcy straightened his coat.

Fitzwilliam strode toward them. "I imagine it will be at least several days before it is safe to travel again."

Darcy grumbled under his breath.

"I know you do not like delay, but I see little alternative." She slipped her hand into Darcy's crooked arm.

"Now you see the value of a broad acquaintance, eh Darcy?" He tilted his head and winked. "Without it, we could be spending the evening and the day ahead at an inn."

"And if we had relied upon your broad acquaintance, we would be." Darcy's eyebrow rose.

Liza snickered under her breath. Darcy would never have made such a remark prior to meeting her. Now he was acting—or at least starting to act—like a

Fitzwilliam brother. It took some getting used to.

Perhaps that was part of the reason Father liked Liza so. Even Mother conceded she had her amenable qualities.

She urged them toward the stairs.

Knightley met them in the still over-warm parlor where the Elliots and Bennet awaited. A bead of sweat trickled down the side of Sir Walter's face.

Bennet sported that look he wore around Collins. Did he find Sir Walter as amusing—or as annoying—as Collins? Either was equally possible. Could there be two such ridiculous men in England?

"Mrs. Knightley has already taken her father into the dining room. Shall we follow?" Knightley gestured toward the door.

Mr. Woodhouse sat comfortably at the foot of the table, a loin of pork nearby. Mrs. Knightley presided at the head of the table and acquainted her guests with the various dishes as they sat down.

Her staff deserved praise for pulling together a worthy menu in spite of the short notice and weather, which must have prevented garnering additional supplies. How much credit was due to the housekeeper and how much to Mrs. Knightley? Despite her apparent youth, perhaps there was more to her than first glance would suggest.

Even Sir Walter did not turn up his nose at the courses before him. What greater praise might there be?

Mr. Woodhouse shaved an irregular slice off the pork, his hand shaking so much it was a wonder that the meat was the only thing he cut. He handed Knightley the cutlery. Mrs. Knightley breathed a sigh of relief.

So did Liza.

Someone had once told him that the Chinese did not place knives on the dinner table because it was not a place for weapons. Perhaps they had a point.

A footman brought a plate of gruel and placed it before Mr. Woodhouse.

He leaned back a bit and smiled. "Would anyone else like a plate? Mr. Bennet, Sir Walter, perhaps? My cook makes a most tolerable gruel."

"Gruel, sir?" Sir Walter's nose wrinkled.

"Indeed, most healthful for the digestion, you know. I do not at all understand the appeal of so large a meal so late in the day."

"Your concern for our health is most gracious." Bennet took several slices of pork. "I imagine, Sir Walter, you do not indulge in a great deal of gruel."

The footman brought the platter of pork to Sir Walter. "By no means, I think it only appropriate for the sick room."

Miss Elliot gasped and colored. She sipped her wine, probably to hide her face.

"I imagine it provides a soothing respite from the taxing variety of rich menus." How did Bennet keep a straight face saying such a thing?

"It does indeed, sir." Woodhouse lifted a trembling spoon.

"Whilst that might be so," Fitzwilliam caught Miss Elliot's eye and gestured to the nearby platters. She nodded, and he served her dainty portions of each. "I am still of a mind and appetite to prefer heartier victuals."

"Young men usually are," Woodhouse murmured over his spoon.

"I suppose your refined connections influence

your tastes." Bennet lifted his wineglass toward Fitzwilliam.

"More likely his stays in His Majesty's army." Knightley tipped his head. "I have heard officers enjoy very sophisticated tastes."

Fitzwilliam snorted and rolled his eyes.

Best refrain from further comment.

"Now that you have an estate, will you continue in the army?" Miss Elliot asked.

"I had thought to stay in until I became a general—it is so much finer a title than colonel."

Liza and Darcy exchanged creased-brow glances. Perhaps that level of sarcasm was not necessary. Miss Elliot had no idea of his experiences nor his opinions.

"In my opinion, colonel is quite as fine a rank as a naval captain. Quite as acceptable. My daughter is married to a Captain Wentworth, brother to Admiral Croft, you know. Excellent connections, both of them."

But then again, in the baronet's company, perhaps a healthy dose of sarcasm was essential. "I am pleased you approve of my rank, but I doubt I will retain it much longer. I expect I will have to sell out soon to manage Listingbrook."

"Will you miss the army?" Was Miss Elliot trying to antagonize him? Her expression seemed very sincere but …

"I think not." Enough said.

Quite enough.

Sir Walter drained his wineglass and piled more pork on his plate. "I should think a young man like yourself would miss the rigors of military life."

"But it is so dangerous. How could a sensible man relish that?" Woodhouse's spoon clattered against his plate.

"Do you miss the quiet of country life now that you are in the smart society of Bath?" Bless Bennet for distracting the conversation.

"Not at all." Sir Walter sniffed.

Of course, after being forced to retrench, he could hardly admit dissatisfaction, could he?

"At times, I do." Miss Elliot looked away.

Sir Walter's eyes bulged, and his face flushed. He did that a great deal. Perhaps he should consult an apothecary about whatever condition caused it.

"So much society can be exhausting at times. Sometimes one longs for the quietude of one's own home." Miss Elliot pushed bits of potato around her plate.

She dared disagree with her father in company? The woman had a spine.

Singular, indeed.

"Is that what brings you here to the quiet of our fine countryside?" Knightley gestured for the footman to refill the wineglasses.

Sir Walter pulled himself up a little straighter, his nose in the air. "We are on our way to visit our cousins the Dalrymples at their home. The Dowager Lady and her daughter."

Miss Elliot's lip curled as she sipped her wine. Her father might not have seen the gesture, but Fitzwilliam did. He had little affection for the Dalrymples. They had no sense of humor to note. What did Miss Elliot dislike about them?

Mr. Woodhouse dabbed his chin with his napkin. "I do not think much of traveling to see people. Travel occasions all manner of danger from weather and highwaymen and accidents. Oh, I read of the most dreadful accident involving a post coach recently."

"I believe I read the same account. Entirely shocking. You might be surprised to hear I do not favor travel myself. It is only that my son Darcy is so persuasive that I am here at all." Bennet winked at Liza.

"Please do not mistake my father's reticence for travel to suggest you are in any way unwelcome. We do enjoy entertaining guests so very much." Mrs. Knightley rang a silver bell for the servants. "Shall we ladies repair to the drawing room and allow the men their port?" She rose and led the ladies out.

Miss Elliot trailed half a step behind, shoulders straight and chin up. She really did have an elegant figure.

Elizabeth pulled her shoulders back and lifted her chin. No one would have the satisfaction of seeing her walk with anything less than perfect dignity. Still, it was humiliating that the highest ranking woman, the baronet's daughter, should have to follow the married women out of the room.

Mrs. Knightley seemed artless enough, not up to such subtle machinations. What was more, she had little need to lord her superiority over her guests, not when constantly plied by the obvious adoration of her husband and father.

Lady Russell warned that jealousy was unbecoming—and obvious. Probably best keep that advice in mind.

Coffee and biscuits awaited them in the drawing room. No doubt Mrs. Knightley had been given free rein with the room's décor. Far more feminine and delicate than the rest of the house, it was what a drawing room should be. Fine fabrics—if a touch older—furniture arranged for conversation, interesting bric-a-brac throughout to spur conversation. Very well thought out to promote the comfort of her guests.

The china service was particularly tasteful, handed down from mother to daughter, perhaps even grandmother to daughter and granddaughter. The entire room had a quaint, elegant feel, a little like tea with the Dalrymples.

Somehow that was comforting.

They sat around the tea table as Mrs. Knightley served them.

"Darcy tells me you have not been married very much longer than we have." Mrs. Darcy stirred sugar and cream into her coffee.

"We married just over a year ago, now." Mrs. Knightley straightened her skirts just a bit. "Sometimes it is still hard to believe. I never truly thought I would marry, you know. Papa would not have been able to tolerate me leaving him to live all alone at Hartfield."

"My father does not much like change, either. He does not admit it readily, but I am quite sure he misses me at home. I cannot think of another reason why he would have visited Pemberley three times in the fifteen months we have been married."

"How fortunate for you that he is willing to travel. I do not think Papa will ever go beyond Highbury again. But he is content and has many friends here. I think they would be alarmed to see him leave for any reason."

No one could have said that about Father at

Kellynch. No one had seemed melancholy to see the family depart. Did Anne realize that was the reason why she left the take-leave visits for Anne to accomplish? Probably not.

"No doubt Longbourn village has been very surprised at Papa's new habits." Mrs. Darcy nibbled the edge of a macaroon. "Oh, these are delightful. My mother's cook used to make some like these, but Mrs. Reynolds at Pemberley cannot seem to make them come out like this. Do you have a receipt I could copy?"

"These are my father's favorite. They are the only biscuit he will eat without worry about his digestion. He will be only too happy for me to share the receipt with you. In fact, I believe he would insist." Mrs. Knightley giggled.

Was this truly all these matrons had to talk about?

"You have a very fine instrument there. Would you mind if I played?" Elizabeth rose.

"Of course, please. I fear I have never been as diligent as I should about practicing. My musical accomplishments are modest at best." Mrs. Knightley gestured toward the pianoforte.

"I confess I am relieved to hear you say that. We shall no doubt be called upon to play for the gentlemen, and I am surely no proficient." Mrs. Darcy smiled.

Lovely, one more thing the local matrons had in common. If they suddenly discovered they liked their morning chocolate with cinnamon rather than nutmeg, she might well flee back into the snow.

She ran her fingers lightly over the keys. The instrument was well-tuned. That was some relief. Just sitting at the keyboard eased her tension and promised a few moments respite from everything she would rather ignore.

How many hours had she spent recently, immersed in the pages of Mozart or Beethoven, music that demanded her entire concentration? Anne still thought it because of the "Elliot pride" that she had to learn the most complex music she could. But Anne was wrong.

Where else could she hide in plain sight, away from Father's folly and the demands of the creditors? It was her refuge, her sanctuary, one that she might even carry with her, as she did now.

Her fingers danced over the keys, playing whatever first came to her. An advanced piece, but not so much so that her hostess should feel intentionally shown up.

The matrons on the couch nodded in time with the music, still caught up in their conversation. Probably trading tips on cleaning silks. How domestic. Would they not be surprised to know that rubbing with warm, dry bran cleaned them very effectively? But they would never take her word on it. What did a spinster know about such things?

They barely looked up from their conversation when she curtsied and made her excuses for retiring. At least they made that easy.

After the ladies withdrew, Knightley produced an excellent bottle of port but no cigars. Mr. Woodhouse declared them vile things indeed.

Sir Walter snorted some kind of complaint under

his breath. Fitzwilliam forced himself not to laugh. He happened to share Woodhouse's opinion.

"So you are very fond of Bath?" Bennet took a heathy draw off his glass. "My wife has, on several occasions, remarked upon her desire to go there herself. She has been told the waters there would do wonders for her nerves."

"She suffers with her nerves, does she?" Woodhouse tapped the table. "My apothecary, Mr. Perry, has an excellent preparation for such things. You might acquire relief from him without the trials of traveling to Bath."

"Do you take the waters at Bath, or perhaps partake of the hot baths?" Bennet asked.

The corner of Sir Walter's lips curled back. "The baths are something of a mixed bag, I would say. I believe they are healthful and excellent for one's complexion. Yet, they are always full of skeletal frights, ridden with some sort of disease. I would be inclined to indulge more often were I not forced to look upon those poor wretches."

Mr. Bennet's brows flashed over his wry smile. "Fascinating observations, sir."

"It might be wise to consider that a great number of those deformed wretches came by their injuries serving on the continent, combatting Napoleon in the service of the King." Fitzwilliam gritted his teeth and clutched the edge of the table.

"Their service is noble to be sure, but what good is their inflicting their disfigurements upon the rest of us?"

Fitzwilliam dug his heels into the thin carpet. His scarred shoulder and thigh throbbed in time with his tense heartbeat. "I am quite certain what should not be inflicted upon us are the new whims of fashion—dandies in breeches so tight that they cannot pick up a dropped handkerchief. Those are the true bane of decent folk."

Of course that was not a comment on the fit of Sir Walter's breeches. Not at all.

Sir Walter sniffed. "So you consider yourself an expert on fashion, sir? I am surprised—"

Fitzwilliam rose before he realized he was moving. "Pray excuse me, Mr. Knightley. I find myself quite fatigued from the day. I believe I shall retire." He bowed.

Darcy looked at him with that overprotective, overbearing Darcy look. At least he understood and would not try to stop him.

He might even take the baronet to task later for his attitude. Under other circumstances, Fitzwilliam might try to discourage Darcy from it. But today, it would be welcome.

"Do you require anything for your comfort?" Knightley rose, his expression mirroring Darcy's.

"Not at all, thank you." Unless he could provide a head full of good sense to the stupid baronet, and considering the look on his face, he probably would have tried. "Good night."

Though Knightley might consider him rude, the risk of giving offense was worthwhile. Another minute in that fool's presence and he would surely say something most untoward.

Mrs. Knightley had shown them a gallery not far from his chambers when she toured the house with them. Though it would not likely be lit now, it was long enough for pacing. That was what he needed.

Moonlight through the windows should provide sufficient illumination for his purpose.

His boots rang against the marble, echoing like a sergeant's voice in the narrow space.

That ninnyhammer Elliot would not survive an hour in combat. He would not even survive training. Probably would have trouble staying on his own horse.

"Oh!"

He jumped back and squinted into the shadows. Miss Elliot sat huddled in one of the hall chairs, a suspicious glisten on her cheeks.

Blast and botheration. Polite company was not what he needed now.

"Pray forgive me for startling you, Miss Elliot. Are you well? Is there something I might do for you?"

She sniffled and dabbed her face with a handkerchief wadded in her hand. "Thank you sir, but there … there is nothing I require."

"You found the ladies' company trying?"

"Mrs. Darcy is all that is gracious, but I often find company trying."

"The company of married woman particularly so?" That was what Rosalind said, at least until her recent marriage.

She gasped and glared at him with eyes that blazed like rifle fire.

"Pray forgive me. I did not mean to offend."

She jumped to her feet and stalked off.

He followed, cutting her off near the window. "Madam, I insist. Truly, I meant no offense."

"What does it matter? I should become accustomed to it." She turned her shoulder to him.

"You sound grievously distressed."

"Indeed I am. But what would you care of it? It is not a matter with which a man of your standing would trouble himself."

"My sisters often found it necessary to confide their troubles to me."

"Indeed, what a singular notion." Her eyes narrowed, and her tone honed to a fine edge.

That kind of a challenge was not the way to dissuade him.

He gestured toward the hall chairs near the wall. "We must have some conversation. And a substantive one is as good as any."

"My father hardly finds it necessary."

"Indeed," he grunted, a sound Mother warned him against in polite company.

"So he offended you—that is why you are here? Pray, do not take your offense out upon me. I am not responsible for him or his ideas any more than Mrs. Darcy and Mrs. Knightley are responsible for their fathers' opinions."

"Worry not. I have a father of my own whose sentiments I often find myself at loggerheads with."

"I am pleased you understand." She rewarded him with a brief glance.

"So, you see I am not some ogre."

"I concede your point."

He held out one of the chairs for her, and she sat. He pulled another chair to sit in front of her. Probably a mite too close, but he had to be able to see her face through the darkness, did he not?

"Are you not looking forward to visiting your Dalrymple cousins?"

She sucked in a deep breath and pressed her fist to her mouth. Her head twitched back and forth. "What do you know of my family, sir?"

Probably best to soften the truth.

"Like many titled gentlemen, debt is an issue. Sir Walter has removed his household to Bath to retrench and restore his affairs to rights. The heir presumptive, a William Elliot, keeps the daughter of the family solicitor under his protection and is not on good terms with the head of his family."

She turned her face away, revealing a striking profile. "A most politic rendition of the tale, to be sure. I had considered Mrs. Clay a friend."

By all rights, Elliot would have done well to have married one of the Miss Elliots. No doubt she felt his defection to her friend bitterly.

"My father is deeply offended by Mr. Elliot's actions, so much so he has been moved to drastic action."

Drastic action often meant a duel, but the baronet did not seem the type. "How so?"

"He means to get himself a son and heir."

"I suppose that would indeed be effective revenge against an heir presumptive." It was a wonder he had not attempted to do so sooner.

"He means to make the dowager Lady Dalrymple's daughter, Miss Carteret, an offer of marriage."

Marrying a cousin was always a convenient solution. Father had once suggested he marry Georgiana.

"You believe his offer will be accepted?"

"I think it quite likely. She has youth and a handsome fortune, and he a title—not as grand as her father's, of course, but no other titled man has made an offer. They are each in want of what the other possesses."

It would not be the first or the last such match to

be made. The gossip pages would hardly notice. "You do not relish the thought?"

She snorted. "Miss Carteret is younger than I! My sister Anne's age if not even younger. Have you any idea of how humiliating it will be to have my place as mistress of my father's house usurped by so young a woman?"

"I have some very good idea of it."

"A bachelor is respectable in all company, but a spinster is a blight on society." She rose and paced along a strip of moonlight.

In the silvery light, her mask of hauteur fell, revealing a handsome woman with elegant bearing and refined features. Her figure was no longer a girl's, but a woman's, one refined under society's fires.

"Forgive me, but your father's attitudes seem a far greater blight to society."

"Then I am doubly cursed."

"That is not what I meant at all to say."

She spun to face him, looking him full in the eye.

Her eyes were deep grey and quite fine.

"Then what did you mean to say?" she whispered.

"I am far more offended by your father's diatribes on the offensiveness of ugliness than a woman …"

"You can say it, on the shelf."

He dragged his hand down his face. "Why do you assume I mean to insult you?"

"Why should I expect anything else? My father, my sisters, even our friend Lady Russell do not hesitate to point out my flaws, however gently they try to accomplish it. I have lost my bloom. I am arrogant. I have expectations set too high—forgive me, I should not speak so." She turned her back, arms wrapped around her waist.

"What do you expect?"

"Not as much as my father used to insist I expect. A companionable man. One with enough rank in society to understand from whence I have come. One with enough that he can be patient in the payment of my dowry, but not so much that he would look down upon me for my father's situation."

"And what have you to offer such a man? You must agree a dowry which may never be paid is a strong disincentive."

"I am well aware of that. But I fancy I can be some asset to a husband beyond a fortune. I am an accomplished woman by society's standards. Since I have taken over the management of my father's household, I can attest to being able to run quite a fashionable household with unexpected economy."

He strode to look at her face to face. "That is indeed a useful accomplishment."

"I am pleased to have your approval."

"You think a bachelor's life far more comfortable? I assure you, if spinsters are leading apes into hell, they will find the bachelors already have a place carved out for them there."

"That is a unique philosophy."

"We single men do not proclaim it loudly, but it is entirely true that a woman's hand is what makes a house a home. That is why I dread taking this estate, despite the fact I should be overjoyed now that I have true means of my own."

"You have no sister, no aunt, no cousin to run your home for you?"

"None. My last remaining sister recently married, and the only spinster aunts I have are not in health enough to keep house. I loathe the notion of being there alone and subject to the match-making machinations of the village matrons and the vicar's wife."

"But did you not say—"

"I do not wish to be some project, some plaything for someone to crow over. I had enough of that in the army. I do not wish to be a pawn in anyone's games anymore."

"It seems we share a common dilemma, sir." She lifted her chin as if daring a rebuke.

"I had come to the same conclusion. I am not one to turn away from what well may be the hand of Providence."

"The hand of Providence?" Her eyebrow rose.

"Perhaps. Since the weather looks like we will be here several more days at least, it seems wise to see if we have the basis for the sort of friendship a married couple should possess."

"You are quite the romantic, are you not?"

"Not anymore, and perhaps not ever. If that is something you expect or require, then that is answer enough to ensure that we should never begin."

She sighed. "At one time, I may have felt that way, but I have no taste for the fancies of romance. I want a home of my own with someone whom I can like and respect."

"So then have we a plan?"

"I suppose so, but…"

He took her hand and raised it to his lips. "Yes, we have violated every ground of propriety in being here and having this conversation at all. So then, why stop? Tell me of your last season in Bath, the entertainments you sought, the society you kept." He led her back to the pair of hall chairs. "We have little enough time to become acquainted with one another. Let us not waste it."

The conversation was awkward at first, but soon she revealed many pleasing opinions and a wicked sense of humor. To be sure, traces of the much-gossiped "Elliot Pride" remained, but it was not far different from the "Fitzwilliam pride" with which he was very familiar and even comfortable, especially from a handsome, articulate woman.

ᎠᏇChapter 3

HOWLING WINDS BUFFETED Elizabeth Elliot's window, shattering away the last vestiges of sleep. Pressing her head into the pillow, she stared up into the bed curtains. Had last night actually happened?

Yes, it had. Colonel Fitzwilliam, second son of the Earl of Matlock, had sat with her half the night, talking almost as old friends might talk. Perhaps he was not as handsome as his cousin Darcy, but he was by far the handsomest man who had paid her any attention since the debacle with Mr. William Elliot.

Her stomach churned. His attentions toward Anne were offensive on so many accounts. They were due her on the account of her being the eldest. But all of that paled in comparison to his taking up with Mrs. Clay.

What a fool she had been to consider "dear Penelope" a friend.

Would Colonel Fitzwilliam prove to be such a friend himself? The Matlocks were known to be a generally discreet family, and there was virtually no gossip concerning the colonel. That fact spoke well of him. If only there were some means for more direct intelligence.

Surely Mrs. Darcy would know. There had to be a way to get her opinion of her cousin in some candid moment.

By no means did he appear to be perfect. Years in the army had knocked away some of the polish a peer's son usually displayed. His opinions were forceful, and a powerful core of stubbornness ran through him. But he was also a principled man. He understood her and was willing to offer respect in a way her father never had. There was much about him that reminded her of Wentworth.

Anne and her husband loved one another. Could she love the colonel, and he her? Did it matter, though?

Compatibility and friendship were far more significant concerns. Those were the things that would last.

To discern their potential for those, she had to spend time with him, something she could not do whilst lying abed. Where was her abigail?

Could he afford for her to retain her lady's maid? Surely, he would not expect her to do without. Did he keep a valet? Perhaps her maid could find out—yes, that was exactly what she must do.

As she dressed, she instructed her maid on seeking the necessary information.

"And what if there should be questions about you, Miss? How do you wish me to respond?" Her abigail tucked a wool shawl around her shoulders.

How indeed?

Impressions ought to be managed most carefully, especially with so much on the line. But then again, that was the game William Elliot had played with her. She worked her tongue against the bitter taste along the roof of her mouth. "Offer the truth. I do not wish to have to keep track of what details might be invented."

"But it might not be complimentary."

Fitzwilliam was too shrewd to believe something too sugar-coated.

"Be as generous as possible, but do as I instruct."

The maid curtsied and left, probably wondering what had come over her mistress.

So did she.

Despite the howling winds and driving snow, warmth suffused her. How long had it been since a man had paid attention to her, even if it was in a most business-like fashion? She could even face the matrons of the house with genuine equanimity today.

No wonder Anne had blossomed so under Wentworth's attentions. The sense of being wanted, or even possibly wanted, was positively intoxicating.

She made her way into the morning room. Pray let him be there!

A cheery fire on one side of the room and candles on the other lit and warmed the small chamber. The yellow paper hangings and gold damask curtains glowed in the light. A fragrant assortment of lovely, freshly-baked things, ham, and potatoes filled the oblong table to nearly overflowing.

Mr. Darcy, Mr. Knightley, and Colonel Fitzwilliam sat along one side. Mrs. Darcy and Mrs. Knightley on the other both engaged in some kind of decorative sewing. So very domestic.

Elizabeth hated sewing.

"Good morning, Miss Elliot." Fitzwilliam rose and bowed from his shoulders. "Do be good enough to sit here with us. We are reviewing information pertaining to my new estate, and I was just thinking how valuable a woman's perspective would be."

The Darcys exchanged glances that could only be called astonished.

"I would be most honored." She went to the chair he held for her.

"Might I serve you some breakfast?

"That would be most kind."

Odd, Knightley shot his wife a severe glance, but she touched her chest and shook her head.

Fitzwilliam served her dainty, ladylike portions of everything, just as he did the previous night. William Elliot had done that, too, but never asked first. He simply heaped the nearest items on to her plate.

"My solicitor has sent me an inventory of the house, but I am afraid it is a bit difficult for me to sort out exactly what to make of it. Might you be able to assist us?" He slid several sheets of paper toward her.

Hopefully, he did not think himself subtle.

But it was a reasonable test. She scanned the neatly written pages.

"It is not possible to judge the condition of the furnishing by this list, of course. It would appear this is a house more than modest but less than grand. Seven bedrooms and a nursery, and several attic rooms for servants. Not quite as much linen as perhaps there should be, but enough to serve immediate needs. The kitchen seems well furnished, though your benefactor seems to have had a fondness for drinking games."

Fitzwilliam cocked his head and blinked. "How do you gather that?"

She pointed to a line on the inventory. "When one has a collection of puzzle jugs this large, one generally uses them for such amusements."

Knightley chuckled. "She has a good point. And she is right. Markham was known for those games."

"At least I know there is a ready cure for boredom should it strike." Fitzwilliam shrugged. "Have you any thoughts on the necessary number of house servants to manage such a household?"

"In addition to your own man, a cook, housekeeper and maid are essential. To begin, I think an additional maid of all work would be necessary."

"Mrs. Darcy suggests two such maids more appropriate." Fitzwilliam glanced at her, but she did not look up from her sewing.

"Forgive me, Mrs. Darcy, for disagreeing. With only a bachelor living in the house, I think a single maid sufficient, particularly as many of the rooms are kept closed. If Colonel Fitzwilliam is of a mind to do much entertaining, an additional girl might be hired as necessary."

Mrs. Darcy lifted her gaze and nodded, eying Fitzwilliam narrowly.

Father sauntered in, not a hair out of place. "I had no idea you would break fast so early."

"Country hours are on the whole earlier than those kept in town," Darcy muttered over his coffee cup.

"Fashionable hours can be kept anywhere." He seated himself beside Elizabeth. "What was this talk of servants I heard?"

"We were just noting different styles of house-keeping and how they call for different allocations of servants." Mrs. Darcy returned to her stitchery.

Father flicked his hand. "Disagreeable nuisances if you ask me. Always running off and leaving the house understaffed. Seems there could be some way to better manage the rubbish."

Elizabeth blushed. He constantly insisted on hiring more servants than they could afford. That drove her to tell him they had run off when in fact she had to dismissed those for whom they could not find the blunt to pay for.

If this conversation continued, she would probably say something that she would regret very soon.

"Pray excuse me." She left the morning room.

Several steps down the corridor, she stopped. Away from Father had been her only destination. Where to go now? She had just been abominably rude to her hosts.

"Are you well, Miss Elliot?" Mrs. Knightley's staccato steps rang out behind her.

"Yes, thank you. Pray forgive me. I—" She bit her knuckle—what could she say that did not imply criticism of her father?

"Keeping house for one's father can be challenging at times, can it not? Especially when he is fastidious in his own ways." Mrs. Knightley smiled, eyebrows raised.

"Yes, it can be. Thank you." Mr. Woodhouse was probably as demanding as a baronet, after his own peculiar fashion.

"If you would like to use the music room at the end of the hall, please make yourself welcome."

"What a pleasant thought. I would like that, thank

you."

Mrs. Knightley curtsied and returned to the morning room. Did she realize the great kindness she offered in simply allowing Elizabeth a little privacy?

It would be to both their credit if she did, so she would.

She wandered the dim hallway toward the music room.

At least Colonel Fitzwilliam's interrogation had been an indirect one. The men were probably unaware of what had transpired between them, but the ladies could hardly have missed it.

Had she passed his test, or was she supposed to wholly agree with Mrs. Darcy? No doubt that woman could manage Pemberley to Darcy's impeccable standards, but she must have a household budget sufficient to the task. Did she know anything about managing with economy and the challenge of keeping up appearances whilst trying to retrench?

Did it really matter though? It was done. Right or wrong, her answer had been given.

A scullery maid scurried past her to light the fire in the music room. How thoughtful of Mrs. Knightley to send her.

Elizabeth drew her shawl more tightly over her shoulders. Another threadbare patch broke open to reveal the fabric of her gown. Thankfully her abigail was skilled at darning.

The music room's chill air nipped at her cheeks and fingertips. She sat at the piano and laid her fingers on the keys. The maid had lit a pair of candles beside the pianoforte, giving the room just enough light to feel intimate.

Too intimate for a concerto.

A soft ballad flowed from her fingertips. She closed her eyes and allowed the music to drown out everything else in her heart and mind.

A throaty bass voice picked up the next measure and added the lyrics of loss and longing. These were not empty words. He knew of what he sang, so intense her fingers almost failed her.

The final chorus faded away, and she dabbed her eyes with her shawl.

"You play very well. Would you play another?" Fitzwilliam words hardly rose above a whisper.

His warm, fuzzy voice tickled the back of her neck, sending tingles down her spine. That did little to help her remember another piece of music.

He chuckled in her ear. No, that did not help either. He reached around her to the keyboard, not embracing her and yet—

"Do you know this?" He played several measures.

Why did he choose that song?

A love song she dared not admit how much she liked. The tingles along the back of her neck prevented her from nodding, so she began to play his suggestion.

He pulled himself straighter and took a half-step nearer. Near enough to feel his warmth behind her, and sang.

He sang well enough to entertain a drawing room, but the feeling he placed in the song—

Oh! She fudged several notes.

He was revealing himself to her just as he had required of her earlier. But the passion in his song was no show for an audience. It reflected the man himself.

She swallowed hard. Such a man might require more than polite interchanges over the dining room table.

Might he look at her as Wentworth did Anne?

Could she bear it if he did?

Her cheeks burned, and her heart raced in a tempo at odds with their song.

She finished the ballad and launched into an aria she had never dared play for an audience. The poignant strains were far too intense for proper company. In the privacy of her own practice, she had sung the words once or twice, but doing so was far too much for today.

He hummed behind her, an occasional word or phrase breaking out.

He knew the lyrics! Prickles coursed down the back of her neck.

As the final strains faded, she peeked up at him. His eyes were closed above a peculiar smile.

"Listingbrook has a pianoforte," he whispered.

It probably would not be polite to remind him that she already knew. It had been listed in the inventory he had shown her.

Soft applause came from the doorway.

"That was lovely, Miss Elliot." Mrs. Knightley entered with the Darcys, Mr. Woodhouse and Father on their heels. "Pray, play us another."

The Darcys sat near the pianoforte while Mrs. Knightley settled her father near the fire.

Father muttered something about not expecting to have to go looking for entertainment.

She started to answer him, but stopped before the first word escaped. What point would there be in that conversation? It would not look well on her, and she never carried a point with him in any case.

Mr. Knightley joined them and suggested she play

something they could all sing with.

She launched into a series of merry folk tunes. Soon most of the room sang along.

The Darcys sang quite well together, but poor Mr. Woodhouse! His voice did not improve for all his enthusiasm. His daughter took after him, poor thing. Perhaps that was why she never applied herself to the pianoforte. But her obvious imperfections did not change the doting looks Mr. Knightley cast her way.

Perhaps not the most refined performance she had ever given, considering Father's expression, but one she would happily repeat just for the joy of it.

Mr. Knightley brought out the card table, and they amused themselves with a game of commerce until Mrs. Knightley suggested that the ladies refresh themselves before a cold luncheon.

Mrs. Darcy caught up with her on the stairs.

"Pray, Miss Elliot, might you accompany me to my dressing room. I should very much like to speak with you for a bit." Her smile was sweet, but something about the strength in her eyes was not.

Still, how could one politely refuse such an invitation?

She followed Mrs. Darcy to her dressing room, steeling herself. How often had she called Anne to her chambers to have a "conversation?"

Mrs. Darcy closed the door behind them. "Forgive me my forthrightness, Miss Elliot, but pray help me understand the nature of your acquaintance with Colonel Fitzwilliam."

"Excuse me, Mrs. Darcy, but I do believe that is his business. He is very capable of managing it himself."

"Of course he is quite capable, but he is very dear

to us, and we are concerned for him.”

So they thought her some sort of mercenary? How lovely.

She counted to ten before answering. “Then perhaps you should bring your concerns to him.”

“Be assured that we will. I cannot help but notice that there seems to be a great deal of attention—”

“Mrs. Darcy, I am not accustomed to being subjected to such impertinent questions.”

“Pray do not be offended. Our concern is—”

Elizabeth wrapped her arms in her shawl and crossed them tightly over her chest. “I can well understand your concern, madam. You have heard of my father’s situation and do not want to see your cousin pursue a fortune that might never be realized.”

“You misunderstand me.”

“No, I am certain that I understand you quite well indeed. I shall not subject myself to any more of this conversation.” She dashed out and down the stairs.

How much distance could she put between herself and that ghastly woman? Perhaps if she stepped outside for just a moment, she might be able to clear her mind.

Sir Walter muttered something about refreshing himself as well and wandered out. After all, sitting about listening to music was a vastly exhausting process.

Bah! His toilette was probably as complicated as Brummel’s. Unpleasant, self-centered, arrogant …

“Forgive me for being so bold, Fitzwilliam, but I must ask. Did my wife have a hand in engendering this musical interlude?”

Fitzwilliam's head whipped around, and he stared, gaping at Knightley. "Excuse me?"

Darcy neither flinched nor blinked. Why was he not surprised by the remark?

Knightley rolled his eyes. "At one time, my wife had a penchant for match-making. After we wed, she assured me that she would leave the practice off all together. I had thought her sincere in her promise."

"So naturally, you assume that finding Miss Elliot and myself in the music room together was the results of her machinations?" He folded his arms over his chest.

"It is not beyond the bounds of imagination."

"And you consider me incapable of out-maneuvering a country matchmaker when I have been foiling my mother's and sisters' attempts all these years?"

"You must admit, it is a bit notable that you are paying such singular attentions to Miss Elliot." Darcy's eyebrow rose.

This was not the first time Fitzwilliam wanted to remove that particular expression from Darcy's face. "And you think me incapable of managing my own affairs?"

"Forgive me if I observe that where females have been concerned—"

Fitzwilliam slapped the arms of his chair. "I fully realize, that I have not been so fortunate as either of you. So good of you to remind me. I am somehow a lesser being because I have not met a woman who proves a match to my heart and soul."

"Richard." Darcy's voice took on the peculiar warning growl.

The one he used when arguments became too personal.

The one that, when they were boys, presaged a round of fisticuffs.

The one he should not ignore.

"Do not take that tone with me, Cousin. You may remove the smug look from your mien as well, Knightley. It is quite bad enough that you flaunt your domestic felicity like a badge of honor. You do not need to peacock about as though it makes you morally superior as well."

Darcy's brows knotted. "This is not at all like you. What is wrong?"

"Must there be something wrong for me to simply be exhausted from married men treating me like a lower class being? I assure you that I would have very much liked to have been married by now, but unlike either of you elder sons, Providence's favor visited elsewhere. But do not mistake my state to be a plea for your advice. Be assured, I remain quite in possession of my faculties and fully cognizant of what is going on around me." He sprang to his feet. "Excuse me now, gentlemen. Enjoy the gentle smiles of your brides."

Darcy sputtered something that he probably should have listened to. But what point in listening to more of the same? When had he asked their opinion on anything?

Darcy had never been so quick to interfere before his marriage. What prompted him to take such liberties now?

Damn the storm, and damn the snow. He needed air and space and was not going to find it in the confines of another man's home.

Just how quickly could he have his greatcoat?

Oh, for a man's greatcoat! Such a garment would have been far better armor against the weather than her own pretty cloak and muff. The wind tore at the edges, driving itself between her and the fur lining in an obscenely familiar sort of way. Elizabeth battled to pull it closer.

From one far too intimate interrogation to another. Why should she expect anything else, though? It seemed the only one who did not entirely ignore her, or treat her with suspicion was Fitzwilliam. In their brief—very brief acquaintance—they had exchanged more true intimacy than she had ever before shared with anyone. Certainly William Elliot had never been so honest with her.

She pulled her muff in tighter to her chest. That held back some of the wind.

Of all people for him to have taken up with—Penelope—her particular friend! Yes, men kept their mistresses, but well away from good company. Then it was tolerable enough—

No, No! She must not cry. Those tears had long since been shed. She forced her feet forward. Best to keep moving in the cold.

Nothing could change what had happened—only what was to come.

If Father did marry Miss Carteret, then perhaps there would be money to pay at least part of her dowry. Perhaps, that might make her a more attractive match for the colonel.

What was she thinking? Had she truly become so desperate? It was too soon. If only there were time to know him better. Even only a few weeks, it might be enough.

Wind swirled about her, scouring her face with bits of ice. Her cheeks ached and burned. Perhaps it would be best to return to the house.

She turned around and peered into the swirling white.

No house.

How odd. She must have gotten turned around. To the right and left, only more gray and white swirls.

Perhaps if she followed her steps. She retreated in her own footprints half a dozen steps before they faded into the same white that enveloped her.

She could not have gone so far from the house, could she?

Damp, aching, numbing cold penetrated her boots, seeping up her ankles into her legs. Moving. She had to keep moving. It was the only source of warmth she had. The house could not be far, and it had to be in the direction she now faced. She ducked her head into the wind and trudged on.

Fitzwilliam paced the vestibule. How long could it take to fetch a man's coat?

At last.

His valet, coat over his arm, hurried toward him.

Who was that in his wake?

"Sir, Miss Elliot's abigail. She says she must speak with you."

The lady's maid curtsied. "Sir, pray forgive me, but Miss Elliot has been gone so long."

"Gone? Gone where?" He forced back the urge to grab the woman by the shoulders and shake her for more information.

"She said she needed air. Demanded her cloak and went outside. But it has been far too long, and the storm has grown worse. I fear she cannot be warm enough and might even have lost her way." She wrung her hands and refused to meet his eyes.

What kind of cruel joke was this? To meet a potential bride one day and to lose her to the weather the next? No, this was not to be borne.

He whipped his coat around his shoulders, his valet scrambling to help. "Tell Knightley and Darcy that I have gone for her. Do you know in which direction she set off?"

"From the garden doors, sir. She said she would stay close to the house."

"Make sure there is plenty of warm water and a hot fire for when we return." He pulled on his gloves and wound his scarf tightly.

Had she no idea of the danger she put herself in? Probably not. She had likely never encountered such a storm before.

The wind buffeted from all sides as he stepped out. A cloak would not be sufficient protection against it.

Hedges surrounded the gardens, so she probably was not too far. Even if she had found one of the gates, she would have recognized it and stayed within. Surely, she had that much sense, given how practical she had shown herself to be during their conversations.

On leaving the house, she would have turned right, as the right-handed were apt to do. If she moved along the house, the fence around the kitchen gardens would have stopped her. Chances were good that she would be contained on that side of the grounds.

Once he found her, if he followed the house and fences, he had a certain path back. The hedges would bring him back to the house. It would not do to add to the casualties.

He trotted along the side of the house, the screaming wind in his ears. The sky brightened and boomed. He dove for the ground, covering his head. Snow melted on his face, against his lips as he gasped for air.

He peeked up. Where were the flashes of gun fire, the stench of blood, the screams of broken men?

Snow, and beyond that, he knew, hedges and the lonely skeletons of bare trees and bushes surrounded him.

No battlefield.

Hartfield. Not France.

Hartfield.

He pushed up from the icy ground and dusted himself, shoving back a vague sense of cowardice and humiliation. Not the first time, thunder had sent him diving for cover.

Probably not the last, either.

What would Miss Elliot think of him for it? Would she deem him cowardly or perhaps merely daft? Most people's responses were evenly split. Father thought him a coward. Mother, daft. Thankfully his sisters did not know, and his brother never remarked on it.

Darcy and Liza were the only ones who saw it otherwise. Their compassion was not condescending. They never questioned his reasons for reacting as he did. He did not know for certain, but Liza had probably tried to explain to Mother, but a countess did not often listen to those below her, even if they were related by marriage.

He trudged several more steps and, cupping his hands around his mouth, bellowed. "Miss Elliot!" in the lowest tones he could manage, tones less likely for the wind to carry away.

The wind roared a reply.

He resumed his trot, cheeks burning in the scouring wind. Snow had slipped inside his greatcoat and melted, trickling cold down his chest. Wet patches at his knees chilled and spread their misery along his legs. The familiar ache in his shoulder and thigh reminded him that he would pay for this adventure in the coming days.

He stopped at the hedgerow. "Miss Elliot! Miss Elizabeth Elliot!"

Why had he called her Christian name? Perhaps it would get her attention?

Foolish.

He set off again.

Was that—no, wait—perhaps.

He took three steps away from the hedge. The snow was disturbed, trampled and swirled. Perhaps by a lady's cloak.

"Miss Elliot!"

Was that a voice? He could not risk losing his landmark if it was not.

"Call to me—Miss Elliot."

He held his breath.

Bloody—

"Fitzwilliam." The cry was weak, close to the ground.

"Again!" He bellowed and closed his eyes, turning his head toward the sound.

"Here."

Ahead and to the left. He counted steps.

Five. Ten.

"Miss Elliot!"

"I am here."

Ten more steps left.

A dark form, strewn with snow, lay crumpled before him.

Five more steps, running, heart pounding loudly enough to drown out the wind.

"Are you injured?" He knelt beside her.

She looked up at him, face red, shivering. Snow clung to her hood and muff—effective camouflage when she least needed it.

"I slipped and turned my ankle." Her teeth chattered as she pushed herself up.

He hunkered down and opened his greatcoat, drawing her close and wrapping her in the heavy wool. She clung to him, shaking so hard that she nearly off-balanced him.

"Can you walk if I support you?"

"I think there is little choice." Snow fell from her hood as she nodded into the hollow of his shoulder.

"Put your arm around my shoulder."

She slid her arm along the inside of his coat, and he wrapped his around her waist. Holding her close and tight, he pushed them both upright.

She gasped but held fast. It was slow going, but she managed to match his steps.

He counted under his breath. Where was that damnable hedge?

He was off somehow—what had he missed? He paused and squeezed his eyes shut. She huddled closer.

Of course. His steps were shorter now with her.

Another dozen steps perhaps? He urged her into motion.

Ten steps brought them to the hedge.

He exhaled heavily. "Now we have a guide back to the house. I am not sure it is the shortest way, but it is the surest."

She sniffled. "Thank you. I should not have come out."

"No, you should not. Why did you?"

She cringed a little. "I could not tolerate a moment more of your Mrs. Darcy's interrogations. She fancies me some horrid husband hunter, I think."

Laughter welled in his belly and forced him to stop his march.

"Why is that so humorous?"

"A similar conversation with Darcy forced me out as well. That is when your maid shared the intelligence of your absence."

"You cousin does not approve of me?"

"He is high-handed and meddling in affairs he does not understand. I did not seek his opinion, nor do I welcome it."

"Fitzwilliam!" Why did Darcy choose that moment to appear?

"Here!" He turned and waved.

Darcy and two footmen carrying blankets rushed toward them.

"Go find Knightley, and tell him they are found."

The smaller of the two men ran off, following the hedge back toward the house. They wrapped her in the blankets. Darcy and the footman linked arms to form a sort of chair to carry her back, with Fitzwilliam trailing behind them.

It should be him helping Darcy, not the footman. He sighed. Her arm around his shoulders had been pleasing.

❧Chapter 4

DARCY AND THE FOOTMAN brought her into the kitchen, abuzz with activity. A huge fire blazed in the fireplace.

Warm.

The room was warm. Not a bit of wind swept away the delicious, intoxicating heat.

Her abigail and the housekeeper peeled away her cloak and the snowy blankets, replacing them with ones warmed by hot bricks. They settled her into a chair near the fire and pressed a bowl of hot broth into her hands.

"You must drink this," her maid whispered. Even her throaty French accent felt warm. "It will help to drive away the chill."

Elizabeth's hands shook so hard that she dare not drink it yet, so her maid held her hands, and helping her to bring it to her lips. Oh, but it tasted hot and soft and carried heat into her innermost places.

Broth was highly underrated.

Her abigail took the empty bowl.

Mrs. Knightley burst in, Mrs. Darcy on her heels.

"Thank heavens you are safe!" Mrs. Knightley rushed to her side. "We were so frightened for you."

"I am sorry for having given you unease." Her hands shook a mite harder.

"You should get out of your wet things as quickly as possible." Mrs. Darcy's whisper suggested she had far more to say. Probably nothing Elizabeth wanted to hear.

"Of course, she is right." Her maid jumped into action.

Elizabeth bristled, but she was shivering too hard, and her teeth chattering too fast to raise a protest as her abigail helped her to her room. Would that Mrs. Darcy ever stop being so overbearing?

How difficult it was to climb stairs when shivering so hard and struggling not to slip in her wet shoes. Thankfully the colonel was not about to observe her trek. Where was he?

A blazing fire had been laid in her room, and the bed was piled with towels and blankets. Her maid wrapped a warm towel over her hair and began peeling away wet layers and helping her don dry ones. A wrapping of warm blankets followed.

Most times the assistance was a luxury, but today, her hands shook too hard to have managed any of it herself. Finally, her abigail helped her to sit near the fire and wrapped bricks in towels to prop up her feet.

Oh, heavens! Her toes ached and burned as feeling returned to them.

Her maid unwrapped her hair and freed it from its pins.

"You sent the colonel out for me?" Was that unladylike croak her voice?

"Yes, Miss, I did. I did not know what else to do. You had been gone so long. Since he was going out himself, it did not seem like an imposition upon him. I pray I have not angered you." She ducked and cowered slightly.

It was not as if Elizabeth was in the habit of striking her. Was this demonstration really necessary? Or did she think it an appealing show of deference? Father probably favored such things.

"You did well. His assistance was most welcome."

The maid checked a pot on the hob. "Shall I send for some wine to help warm you and some honey for your throat?"

"Yes, do that. Have you spoken to the colonel's valet?"

"I have, on several occasions now." She rang the bell for the maid.

"Was he willing to answer your questions?" Elizabeth bit her lip.

"Not at first, to be sure. It took a bit of convincing, and not in the way you might expect. In particular, he wanted to understand your motive for the questions. He is rather protective of his master."

"It seems that everyone around him is rather protective of him."

"If I may be so forward, Miss, I think it is from genuine affection for him. They do not seem concerned that he is incapable in himself."

It was awfully forward, but useful information nonetheless. To be able to draw so much affection to one's self did speak well of one's character, so it was favorable news as well.

"So then, what did you discover?" Elizabeth tipped her head back as her maid brushed her hair.

"With respect to his financial state, he has an allowance from his family, that is not large enough to support a wife and family in the way a gentlewoman would be accustomed. But with the payment from his sell-out, and the estate he has inherited, he will be able to live as a gentleman, with a family. His tastes do not lean toward extravagance, but he prefers to live 'decently,' in the words of his valet."

And "decently" certainly meant maintaining a lady's maid.

"Debts?" The dreaded word nearly stuck in Elizabeth's throat.

"His valet is not aware of any debts that he owes."

She turned to look her maid in the eye. "That can hardly be possible. What gentleman in his circumstances has no debt?"

The maid cringed a little. "That is not to say he has never had debt, but rather that he has paid it all off. Before his last assignment to France."

Elizabeth studied her maid's face. "There is more. What are you not telling me?"

"His valet has confided that the war changed him. That was why he paid off his debts before he left. He was not sure he would return and did not want to leave 'a mess' behind for his family to tend."

"That does not sound like a wholly disagreeable change."

"If that were the only thing, perhaps not. But there is more. He has been injured, seriously. More than once. I have heard tell of extensive scars that still give him pain."

Father would find his wounds unpleasant, but when would he ever have the chance to see them? He could probably go his whole life never knowing of the colonel's disfigurement.

The more important question was how did she feel about them? Since they were invisible under his clothes, it would be easy to forget about them. He might prefer to keep them covered, so she might may never even see them.

But then again, he might insist otherwise. In all likelihood, they were likely most unsightly. Then what?

Then what indeed?

"They do not seem to impair him though, at least not to his valet's knowledge." The maid rubbed her hair with a towel.

Nor to her experience; there was no doubt as to his strength, not after today. There was such security in his embrace. "That is welcome news. What else?"

"He is considered a genial companion, and has many friends and connections. It seems he is welcome in nearly every good house in London. He often has more invitations than he can accept during the Season and to country estates beyond the Season."

That should suit Father very well.

She began to plait Elizabeth's hair. "He is closest to Mr. Darcy, though, and he relies heavily on Mr. Darcy's opinion."

"That is to say that if I do not have Mrs. Darcy's approval ..." Elizabeth muttered under her breath.

She nodded fractionally. "He is not so dependent, though, that he refuses to make a decision without Mr. Darcy's approval."

Good news, but little surprise. Fitzwilliam did not seem the indecisive type.

"You are still hiding something from me. Is there another woman he is courting or one his family is forcing on him? A mistress, perhaps?"

"No, Miss, nothing so ... simple as that." She tied off Elizabeth's braid and tossed the used towel onto the pile of other wet things. "His man said that since returning from the war, he is altered. Not anxious precisely, but there are things that disturb him unnaturally. Like gunfire—he does not hunt anymore."

"Surely that is not so unreasonable, or at least it does not seem so to me." If he had been wounded, it only seemed natural that gunfire would be unsettling.

"But not just gunfire, anything that sounds like it, such as thunder, trees falling, or fireworks, tends to perturb him greatly. He has dreams, nightmares that leave him pacing the halls in the night. Anything French, even my accent, Miss, can unexpectedly upset him."

Elizabeth snorted. "We both know that the accent is not real. You may easily drop the affectation."

She gasped. "Yes, Miss Elliot."

The maid came with wine and more blankets. She scooped up the pile of wet things and scurried back out.

Her abigail poured a glass of wine and hot water and pressed it into her hands.

Oh, that was the thing. The final tendrils of cold fell away, and at last every bit of her was warm— deliciously, delightfully warm. Her eyelids drooped.

So much to think about, but it could wait.

A clock's chime woke her. She pushed up on her elbows, but the blankets were far too heavy, and she fell back again. Every joint protested, and her head pounded in time. She licked chapped lips. Oh, her throat—as raw as butcher's meat.

What a fine thing when there were important conversations to be had.

"Miss?" Her abigail approached and laid a cool hand on her forehead. "You are feverish."

"How long?" She croaked like the old beggars near the hot baths.

"You have slept nearly a whole day. The colonel asks after you every few hours."

"And Father?"

The maid cleared her throat. "He is in a bit of high dudgeon."

Elizabeth fell back on her pillows. Of course he would be. A cold left one's nose red and one's complexion quite faded.

"The storm let up some hours ago. Mr. Woodhouse sent for the apothecary. He should be here soon."

No doubt with pills and potions to ply. Another bill to pay.

A soft rap at the door drew the maid away, and Elizabeth drifted off to sleep.

The clock chimed again. How long had it been? She rolled to her side and pushed halfway up.

"It is nearly four o'clock." Mrs. Darcy's voice was gentle, appropriate for the darkened room and the pounding in her head. "Fitzwilliam insisted on knowing your condition more directly—he thinks your maid too discreet. I took her place when she went to the kitchen to prepare you a tray. The apothecary insisted you should be awakened to eat." Mrs. Darcy poured half a glass of wine and added hot water.

It did not burn nearly so much as the last time she drank. How could she manage to eat?

"I believe Mr. Woodhouse ordered an extra portion of gruel prepared for you tonight." Mrs. Darcy cocked her head, her voice smiling just a mite.

"He is too kind," she croaked. "Colonel Fitzwilliam?"

"He has a constitution of iron and a will to match. He is quite well, if rather ill-tempered at the moment. I find he is impatient with that which he cannot order about to his liking. Your illness is most definitely not to his liking."

Had she felt a little less dreadful, the implied compliment would have made her blush. She returned the wineglass to Mrs. Darcy's hands and fell back into her pillows. Mrs. Darcy returned to the nearby chair.

No doubt the room would fill with an awkward silence now—or questions which might well be more awkward. Perhaps she might feign sleep.

"Forgive me if I presume too much, but I fear you misunderstood me earlier."

She turned and stared at Mrs. Darcy. Though her face was partly in shadow, there was no reproof or mocking to be found on her features.

"I meant no ill-will toward you. Perhaps you are unfamiliar with mine and Mr. Darcy's story, but my own fortune was quite insignificant compared to what a man of his standing should have sought. I do not judge a woman's suitability by her fortune alone."

Now her stomach felt sick, too. "Then what … what were you trying—"

"Fitzwilliam is like a brother to us. We only want to see him happily settled."

"Then let him choose how that is to happen."

"Rightly said. You cannot blame us, though, for taking notice when he acts so decidedly unlike himself. He is very cautious among ladies, never exerting himself so much to please."

"You think him disingenuous?" Elizabeth propped herself up on her elbows.

"Quite the opposite. We do not wish to see him hurt."

"Nor do I. He is unlike any man of my acquaintance. I should like to know him better."

Mrs. Darcy stroked her chin and looked away. "I am sorry. I expect now that the storm has abated, we will leave soon. Perhaps tomorrow or the next day."

Elizabeth's eyes burned, and overflowed down her cheeks. She bit her lip and held her breath, but it did not help.

Not at all.

She quaked with the effort to hold back the sobs.

Mrs. Darcy pressed a handkerchief into her hands and tiptoed out.

Perhaps she was not such a harridan after all.

When was the last time she had cried? The evening after Anne's wedding. It was all too much to bear. But she had picked herself up and made a good go at things since then.

It must be the exertion and the cold that had her at such loose ends now. She could, she would rally again.

Her abigail entered quietly, bearing a tray, Father a step behind her. She scurried about the room, lighting several more candles. Father's face came into focus.

High dudgeon, indeed.

He leaned into her face, squinting. "You are an absolute fright. Shocking complexion. Your skin is quite scoured raw."

"Thank you. I am feeling a little better, I think." She turned aside.

"Perhaps Mr. Perry's tinctures will improve your color. He certainly left a goodly number for your treatment."

She clutched her forehead.

He flicked his hand. "None of that whining about the cost. Woodhouse insisted."

No point in discussing what was now done. She forced her chapped lips shut.

"Mr. Perry seems to think you should keep to bed a fortnight. Ridiculous! Ridiculous! Lady Dalrymple expects us today. No doubt she will understand about the storm, but they have invited us to travel into town with them. We cannot cause them to delay their plans because you have been foolish enough to catch a trifling cold." He huffed and backed away. Father did not like to be in the presence of illness.

"I would not have caught it if it were up to me."

"I insist ... I insist ..." His face turned red, and he sputtered.

"What would you have me do?" Sitting up so suddenly did nothing to improve her thundering headache.

"Whatever is necessary for you to be able to leave here tomorrow or the next day at the latest. I require you to be recovered."

"And how am I to accomplish such a task?" Shouting—or at least the attempt-- was a poor idea indeed, leaving her throat burning and head pounding.

"How am I to know? That is the apothecary's business. Follow Perry's instructions and see that you are well soon. I will have it no other way." He turned sharply and stomped out of the door.

For all sister Mary's complaints about the Musgroves, she had life on very easy terms compared to living with Father.

Fitzwilliam paced the hall. It was wholly improper to eavesdrop. A despicable, low-class practice at best. But it was often the only way a younger son came to know anything important in the household. Besides, it was not considered eavesdropping if the shouting could be heard across the hall.

Sir Walter was truly a product of his class—selfish, self-centered, and arrogant. At their worst, neither Father nor Andrew was so intolerable. Even Aunt Catherine would find her match in this impertinent baronet.

Oh, that was a thought, the two of them in the same room together.

A door slammed, and footsteps stomped in his direction.

He intercepted Sir Walter halfway down the corridor, near the great stairs.

"Excuse me, sir. You will permit me to pass." Sir Walter sidestepped him, but Fitzwilliam blocked his progress.

"After we have had a conversation."

Sir Walter's face shifted through several permutations, settling upon something eager, like a dog hoping for scraps. Did he expect an invitation to Matlock or some other favor from Fitzwilliam's hand?

"Shall we avail ourselves of the small parlor?" Sir Walter gestured toward a nearby door.

Good idea. Best not to have this conversation for the whole house party to observe. It was enough that they would be able to hear it through the walls.

He extended an arm toward the door. Sir Walter puffed out his chest and sauntered to the sitting room.

Peacock.

Fitzwilliam shut the door behind him, not that it would contain the conversation any more effectively than Miss Elliot's bedroom door had, but it would be a sign to keep others away.

The small parlor was just that, small. Cold sunlight filtered through frosty windows, painting the room in awkward streaks and shadows. Chill air caught him across the face; no fire had been lit there. But they would not be there long enough to require one.

Sir Walter stood in the sunbeam in the center of the room and straightened his jacket. "What may I do for you, Colonel?"

That smile needed to be removed from his self-important face.

Self-control, Fitz.

The general was right. It did not serve his purpose to come out temper flaming. He could—and should—reserve that for when it would work in his favor.

Fitzwilliam clasped his hands behind his back and summoned his command voice. "Ordinarily I am not in the habit of asking favors, but in this case, there is indeed something you may do for me, sir."

"I am at your service." Sir Walter tipped his head just a mite.

Insufferable.

"I am a military man and not accustomed to subtleties, so I will come straight to the point. Your disgraceful displays of pique at your daughter are ungentlemanly and beneath you. You must cease immediately."

Sir Walter's brow drew into tight lines, the kind he decried when others wore them. "What were you doing listening in on a conversation to which you were not invited?"

"You invited the entire household when you began shouting."

"I do not shout."

Yes, he did, and the entire house party would agree.

Fitzwilliam took a step closer and towered over the baronet. "I advise you to treat your daughter with the courtesy and honor appropriate to her station."

"How dare you criticize my manner toward my own family? What business is that of yours? You would do well to attend to your own matters."

"You would do well to concern yourself with something more substantial than mere appearances and your own comfort."

"Are you threatening me?" Sir Walter edged back half a step.

"Should I have to? A true gentleman appreciates wisdom wherever he may find it."

Sir Walter sputtered and grumbled deep in his throat. "You are taking airs you do not deserve."

"You demand respect which you do not deserve."

"Who are you to say what I deserve? I am a baronet."

"And I am the son of an Earl."

"The younger son—"

"Still outranks a baronet—" Fitzwilliam pulled himself up a little straighter.

"—not even his heir."

"Better that than a man who cannot get himself an heir."

"I will not be spoken to in this way." Sir Walter stomped.

"Then do not behave in such a way as to warrant it."

Sir Walter sputtered and turned the color of a dress uniform. He stormed out and slammed the door.

Fitzwilliam eased down against the arm of the couch. That did not go according to plan. But no battle ever did once the enemy was encountered.

What would Miss Elliot think of him? Telling off a woman's father was probably not the best way to win her affection. At least not usually.

He snorted a laugh. It sounded like the sort of thing Darcy would have done—and he had won a woman like Liza.

That was food for thought.

If Miss Elliot turned against him for speaking his mind, it would be telling and best to know it now. He would always be forthright and no one, not even a wife, could ever change that. If she found it intolerable, it would be best for them both to discontinue their friendship.

Was this what courtship was supposed to be—exposing one's flaws and hoping there would not be something the other found intolerable?

All the advice he had ever received insisted that courtship was about putting one's best face on and convincing the other of one's suitability. Nothing had ever come of that, though, so perhaps something different was not so bad a thing.

The door hinges squeaked as the door swung open.

Darcy.

Fitzwilliam rolled his eyes and huffed, looking away. "I suppose you are here to upbraid me for the uproar I have just caused."

"Sir Walter was a bit peeved. I believe my wife has taken it upon herself to calm his temper and soothe his wounded pride."

"She is a good woman."

But Darcy already knew that. It was a reasonable thing to say though.

Careful steps approached, but Fitzwilliam's gaze remained locked on the icy window. The ice and snow probably would not last much longer.

"This is entirely unlike you." Darcy's soft voice came from just behind him.

"I beg to differ. You have been privy to my rather robust conversations with Andrew, even my father."

"I would not call those typical of you. All of those required rather prolonged provocation."

"The baronet is provoking." Fitzwilliam turned to look over his shoulder.

Strange. No judgement marked Darcy's features. If anything he looked … concerned, perhaps even bewildered.

"You are usually far more tolerant of—"

"You are usually far less intrusive." The words came out less forcefully than he had hoped.

"This is not how you react to a single woman, especially one of dubious fortune and average beauty and accomplishments."

"What would you know of it?" He turned his back to Darcy.

"Are you so fond of her after such a very short an acquaintance? Even Collins's acquaintance with Miss Lucas endured several weeks prior to making her an offer of marriage."

"You liken me to Collins?"

"Why are you so intent upon hearing insults?" Darcy planted himself directly in front of Fitzwilliam.

"Why are you so adept at offering them?"

"You have always made a point to be extremely careful where women were concerned. What has changed, and why her?"

"What has changed? Can you not see? Everything—every bloody thing has changed." He threw his hands in the air, nearly striking Darcy. "I have means now. I can support a wife. That has hardly been an option before."

"Then why not seek out someone more agreeable?"

"Because I am not agreeable."

"What are you talking about? Of course you—"

"No, Darcy, I am not." He skirted past Darcy to

pace along the middle of the room. "I am not the man I was. You may thank Napoleon for that. I usually curse him, though, as I have spent the last year coming to grips with the truth. I will never be who I once was. I cannot seek what I once might have. A sweet, young, innocent wife, a child-like thing like Mrs. Knightley who could turn to her husband for all manner of wisdom and strength. I would crush such a soul and I cannot, I will not, do that to another."

"You are being overly dramatic." Darcy blocked his path.

"Who are you to make such a determination when you cannot hear the voices inside my head, pulling and tormenting me. I need a woman who has been tried herself and can stand up to her own demons. How else might she be able to withstand mine?" Fitzwilliam balled his hands into trembling fists.

Darcy edged back a step. "You think Miss Elliot is such a creature?"

"She is the first one of whom I have believed it possible."

"But you do not know?"

"It is hardly possible to be certain in a single day."

Darcy's relief was a little too obvious.

"Why are you so decidedly against her?"

"I am not."

"You make it difficult to tell. I am not a boy, remember. Just because I am unmarried it does not mean I am unwise. I trust that you mean well. But you are overstepping yourself." He stared directly into Darcy's face. Most men could not endure so direct a challenge.

Darcy met his gaze, unblinking.

Stubborn, obstinate, overbearing …

Fitzwilliam turned on his heel and stalked out, nearly colliding with Bennet in the corridor.

"Colonel Fitzwilliam," Bennet tipped his head. "You have the look of a man who has just left a conversation with my son-in-law."

Fitzwilliam stopped and stared. "And what might that look be?"

"Vexed."

He snickered. "He can be high-handed, can he not?"

"You should have heard the way he asked for my daughter's hand."

"I can only imagine."

"It was not as if their courtship was conventional in any sense. I did not even realize it was happening." Bennet smiled that odd little half-smile that Fitzwilliam had not yet worked out the meaning for.

He was an odd man for certain.

"Do you think Liza regretted not having a conventional courtship?"

"My Lizzy? No. Not every woman is, like my wife, in need of public admiration. Just as all are not romantics. Some are satisfied with a comfortable friendship and a peaceful existence. I like to think that is an excellent foundation for a very agreeable match. Jane with her beauty found a more romantical man, entirely to her liking. But Mary and Kitty settled well with companionable men with enough to keep them comfortable and not so much to feed their folly." He cocked his head and lifted an eyebrow just so.

"If it is not too personal, might I ask how long it took you to decide upon marriage to Mrs. Bennet?"

Bennet chuckled. "Deciding and doing were two different things. I should blush to think how quickly I decided—perhaps on our third meeting."

"So soon?"

"It was another six months before I made her an offer."

"Was it time well spent?"

"I think she found it agreeable, but to be honest, I thought it was a waste. Do not tell Lizzy, though. I think she would be quite scandalized to hear it."

Darcy certainly would.

"I can only imagine." Fitzwilliam laughed, tongue firmly in cheek.

"Do not think I recommend haste, but it may not take long for a man to know—and when he does, waiting is a burden." Bennet winked—just barely—and continued on toward the stairs.

Had Darcy—or Liza—set him in place to offer counsel, too?

At least his advice was not nearly as overbearing as Darcy's. And Bennet posed a good question. Did he know yet? No, not quite, but close. Close enough that it should not take very long to come to that place of knowing.

Perhaps, if she felt the same …

He turned on his heel and marched to Miss Elliot's room.

But what would he do once there?

"Oh!"

What was she doing in the hall?

"Colonel?" Miss Elliot looked up at him.

Her hair was pulled into a simple knot, and she wore a very plain dress and shawl—like a woman in her own home, easy and at ease. Except, of course, for her wan complexion and red nose—and even those were a bit endearing.

"Miss Elliot, I had not thought to see you about so soon."

"My father insists—"

"I heard."

She blushed and turned aside.

"Forgive me, but you do not seem well enough to travel."

"His plans are of the utmost importance—"

"To him." He grumbled under his breath.

"—and he insists he cannot be delayed."

"Not even for your health?"

"It is only a small matter. I am sure I will be well enough." She shrugged. It was probably supposed to be a dainty, carefree expression, but came off heavy and worn.

"Do you wish to leave so soon?" He held his breath.

"My wishes are not relevant."

"Perhaps not to him. Do you wish to leave?" He caught her gaze and held it.

One breath, two breaths, three—why did she not answer?

"No, sir, I do not."

He sucked in a deep breath. "I am pleased you are honest with me. I require that."

"What else do you require?" She lifted an eyebrow, a spark returning to her eye.

There was a bit of flirt in her after all.

Good.

Very good.

"Miss Elliot!" Mrs. Knightley, approached with rapid steps, flanked by Liza and Mr. Woodhouse.

"You should not be out of bed, Miss Elliot. Not against Mr. Perry's orders." Mr. Woodhouse worried his hands.

"I thank you for your concern, but my father—"

"I have spoken with him. Indeed, reasoned with him most forcefully." Mr. Woodhouse muttered.

"We all have spoken with him," Liza added, an all too satisfied glint in her eye.

What had she said to him?

"And we have devised a plan which seems most advantageous to all." Mrs. Knightley clasped her hands before her.

Something about the way Mrs. Knightley said the words ... perhaps this was not more bad news.

"If you are agreeable, Miss Elliot, you may remain here at Hartfield for your convalescence. Your father will be free to continue on his travels and return to pick you up on his way back to Bath. I expect it will be several weeks at least, perhaps a month complete."

"Long enough for a complete recovery, I expect." Liza barely winked at Fitzwilliam as she spoke.

Darcy had married a brilliant woman.

"And, Colonel, since your house will hardly be staffed and ready for habitation, Knightley and I insist that you continue your stay with us until you can comfortably take possession—even if it is an entire month or more." Mrs. Knightley glanced back at Mrs. Darcy.

Perhaps the assistance of local matrons did not have to be so very bad a thing after all.

"Darcy thinks it an excellent plan. He fears I may be weary of the privations of travel." She pressed her hands to her belly.

Fitzwilliam's eyes grew wide. "Certainly it will not do to tax you unnecessarily. Your offer is most gracious, Mrs. Knightley, and I would be most grateful to accept." He bowed from his shoulders.

"And you Miss Elliot?"

"Do say you will stay on with us. I shall be so anxious otherwise." Poor Mr. Woodhouse resembled nothing so much as a forlorn hound.

Miss Elliot caught Fitzwilliam's eye briefly. "I should be very grateful for the comfort of Hartfield whilst I recover."

"Very good then. I shall tell Knightley and make arrangements." Mrs. Knightley nodded and headed down the corridor with a swish of her skirts.

"Emma is very good at arrangements." Mr. Woodhouse beamed and followed his daughter.

Liza touched Fitzwilliam's wrist and gazed into his eyes. No doubt she had pleaded his case to Darcy and won him over with those fine eyes of hers—or perhaps her fine wit. Either way, he had an advocate in her. Dear woman.

She nodded. "I shall tell Darcy. I think he will be pleased."

Alone in the hall again, Miss Elliot and Fitzwilliam stared at one another.

"So then, we have a month. Will that be enough?" he asked.

"It is more than I imagined possible. I am hopeful, more than I have been in a very long time."

Oh, the way she looked at him.

He took her hand, cold and soft and small in his, and kissed it. "Very hopeful, indeed."

❧Chapter 5

THE NEXT DAY, Miss Elliot kept to her room, claiming a return of her fever. More likely she was avoiding
her father as he wandered about, declaring that he
was preparing to leave Hartfield. For a few moments,
the colonel was tempted to feel sorry for the man
who seemed barely capable of managing such practical action. How difficult, to be so dependent upon
servants for such basic things.

The urge was short-lived, though, fading into disgust as the baronet berated both his servants and
Hartfield's. No wonder Miss Elliot avoided him.
When at last Sir Walter left, Knightley shut the door
firmly and muttered something under his breath that
sounded alarmingly like "good riddance."

The next morning, Miss Elliot still did not appear.
Was it ungentlemanly to question her absence, now
that they had agreed to a courtship that was to be

conducted in a very short time? Sadly, it was the sort of trick too many women of his acquaintance would readily play with a man.

Apparently, though, Liza wondered as well. She had made a point of sitting with the invalid and reading to her to keep her spirits up. Over luncheon, Liza casually offered her observation that Mrs. Knightley's invitation to stay had been a very good thing. Taking to the road, even in the improved weather, would certainly have turned Miss Elliot's cold into something quite dangerous.

Bless Liza.

It was a maddening tease, though, to have the intent to pursue a courtship only to be stayed by the very reason for the opportunity.

Patience had never been his chosen virtue, though, and that would not change now.

Distraction. He needed some distraction.

There was only one thing to do: apply himself to the estate records supplied by the solicitor. Darcy had been lecturing him on the need to attend to them, so he might as well satisfy his task master.

Dear God, he was truly desperate.

He sat down and stared at the stack of books on the desk. No one could fault Markham's thoroughness. He was more fastidious than Darcy—a fact it would be delightful to point out at the correct moment.

Fitzwilliam leaned back and stretched, trying not to hit the wall behind him. Knightley had been thoughtful, replacing the small writing desk in his room with a more substantial working desk. It had made for a bit of a trial, squeezing his too-tall frame into the limited space between walls and furnishings.

Hopefully the study at Listingbrook would be a bit more spacious.

Listingbrook.

What was he going to do with an estate? It was not as if Father had bothered to teach him anything about land management. His attitude was similar to Sir Walter's: stewards were for that sort of thing.

Now Darcy—and Knightley following Darcy's example—seemed to be trying to pour a lifetime of knowledge and experience into him so fast he gasped for air like a drowning man.

Drowning.

Cold water, closing in, covering over him.

He sprang from his seat and paced the room, gulping lungsful of air as he went. More … more … he needed to breathe.

Air!

He threw open the window. A gust of cold air buffeted his face, burning his lungs. But it was air!

He clutched the window frame, lightheaded, and sagged to his knees.

Forehead against the frigid windowsill, he braced his palms on the floor. There was no water here, plenty of air to breathe.

Must breathe slowly.

Slowly.

He held his breath and counted to five, released the breath over another five counts and breathed in for five more. Again. Once more.

The spots slowly cleared from his vision.

He shut the window and sat, leaning against the wall.

It had been a long time since that memory had intruded.

He raked his hair out of his face.

Did Miss Elliot have any idea of what she might be getting herself into with him?

Certainly not. What lady would expect … this?

She would have to know. Somehow he would have to tell her.

She would probably do the sensible thing and run. She seemed a very sensible woman.

But to fail to tell her would be to entrap her with the same sort of games that he despised.

No, he would not stoop to those means to get a wife. Even if it meant he would be alone.

He trudged back to the desk.

An hour later, he stood and stretched, joints popping, the familiar tearing sensation across his scars reminded him—no, this was not the time for those memories.

What was it about today? It had been months since he had a day as bad as this.

Activity. He must have activity.

Darcy crossed paths with him in the hallway. "Excellent, I was just in search of you."

"That sounds ominous." Fitzwilliam cocked his head and crossed his arms over his chest.

Darcy chuckled.

He was doing that far more now that he was married than he had ever done before.

It was a little unsettling.

"Now that the weather has turned, it would be a good time to see the solicitor in Highbury. It is time to see Listingbrook in the flesh. That is what we came for, after all." A hint of a smile curved Darcy's lips.

That was as close to teasing as he ever came. Sometimes that was disappointing. Right now, it was probably a good thing.

"Capital suggestion. Shall we, then?" He gestured Darcy on ahead of him. Solicitors were usually rather dreadful to meet with: dull, detail-oriented, and without any identifiable sense of humor. Still, it was a useful errand that he might as well get over with.

He mounted his horse and settled into the saddle. He should not dread the solicitor and the ensuing visit to his estate so much. The books revealed a reasonably profitable establishment that had been run well, not some sort of disaster for him to turn around. At least Darcy would tell him so. But it also meant that any credit for success would go to his predecessor, and all blame for failure would fall securely in his lap.

How cynical he had become. When had that happened?

A sharp breeze cut across the back of his neck. He turned up the collar of his coat and hunched a little against the cold.

The wind was very like that on the French plain …

The skin on the back of his neck twitched. Was that the smell of gunpowder?

No, that could not be possible.

He cast about over his shoulder. He and Darcy were alone on the road.

The horse tossed his head. What did it sense? Fitzwilliam's pulse quickened to double time, a low roar in his ears. Cold air burned his lungs, and he dragged in deeper, faster breaths.

"Fitz?" Darcy brought his horse alongside Fitzwilliam's.

Fitzwilliam jumped, and the horse shied. Thankfully instinct was all that was required to bring the creature under control again.

"Are you well?" Darcy's forehead furrowed into deep rows.

Fitzwilliam shook his head. "I am fine, just a bit distracted." He urged the horse to walk on.

Hopefully that would be enough to discourage Darcy. Conversation was the last thing he needed.

They passed quaint cottages, several pleasant farmhouses, and a small pond. A very charming, very comfortable, very English, countryside.

Highbury rose just ahead. How many other English towns looked just like it? Meryton certainly did. Large enough for some commercial interests, some semblance of social life—assemblies, plays, the odd concert or lecture, but nothing to the appeals of London.

Or the expense.

"Will you be happy here? Country life can be rather routine and even a bit dull."

Fitzwilliam looked over his shoulder and stared at Darcy. "Does it really matter? It seems that I now have a home here."

"That is not a foregone conclusion. Though Listingbrook is yours, you do not have to live there. You could lease the house and hire a steward to manage the property for you. You could live elsewhere, off the income from the estate, and not be confined to such limited society. You could take a house in London—"

"I am surprised to hear you say that. You spend little enough time in town."

"You should consider all your options and make the best choice for you, and possibly for the family you might have."

Fitzwilliam stopped his horse and faced Darcy. "You would advise me opposite of your own choices? I find that rather extraordinary. You seem entirely content to spend most of your time at Pemberley."

"I do not recall you being content to keep to Matlock or even Matlock House in London when you had the opportunity."

Fitzwilliam grunted and flashed a tight smile. "So you assumed I had a taste for the wonders of high society?"

Darcy's eyebrow rose in something resembling genuine surprise—not a common expression for Darcy. "Your brothers, Andrew especially, certainly do."

"So, naturally I do as well?" he huffed and looked aside. "I wonder if you know me at all. Perhaps you do not recall, the company at Matlock is not, and has never been, quite as pleasing as the company at Pemberley. Even Rosings Park is an improvement to Matlock."

Darcy's jaw dropped. "I never realized—"

"I suppose it is an easy thing to take for granted when one's own home is peaceful and comfortable. But when it is not, most other places and situations are preferable to staying at home."

Darcy dragged his hand down his face. "Elizabeth understands these things so much better than I."

That was not saying a great deal. Most people did.

"I do not imagine that Pemberley today is much like Matlock."

"It is true what they say about the mistress of a house. Pemberley is not the place you remember under my father. Elizabeth has made it what it once was under my mother's hand: a home. I confess, I did not understand just how much the management of a home would mean to her—or to any woman." Darcy's eyebrows rose.

"What are you so carefully not saying? Just come out with it. I am tired of waiting for you to make your point."

"After we have toured the estate and seen the house, it might be advisable to bring Miss Elliot to visit the property, to see of what she might become mistress."

"And if she does not run away screaming in fright, I should consider that an excellent sign that I should make an immediate offer for her?"

Darcy guffawed and urged his horse into motion once again. After he had pulled far enough ahead that conversation would not be possible, Fitzwilliam followed suit.

Leave it to Darcy to drive home the looming issue that he most did not want to confront.

He never should have suggested a courtship with Miss Elliot, prior to having seen the house. Yes, the books all suggested the estate was in good order and the inventories, even in Miss Elliot's estimates, implied a house that was of suitable size for their needs.

But their needs were not the only consideration. Even with the need to retrench, there was no doubt that Miss Elliot was accustomed to a certain style of life. Had not her father said at dinner the night before he left, "A baronet must be seen to live in a style befitting his rank?"

It seemed to have taken all Darcy's self-control not to contradict Sir Walter. He had said nothing at all for a full hour at least. Bennet had good fun with it, though, baiting the baronet into further and further absurdities, until Knightley interjected himself into the conversation to steer it into safer waters.

Probably a good thing that Miss Elliot had not been present for that show. She would have been mortified at the way Sir Walter droned on and on about the necessity of fashionable drapery in any room that received guests.

Once away from her father, would she expect fashionable draperies?

No doubt they would have to entertain and take their place among Highbury's society. Their home would have to reflect their rank and connections. Was Listingbrook up to the challenge?

If the house was not suitable or the situation entirely disagreeable to her, it would be best to acknowledge it soon and walk away with no hard feelings on either side. There were real limits as to what he could provide her and no telling what she required.

Damn the sliver of hope that taunted him. It was making being practical far more difficult than it should be.

Bloody hell, he did not even know if he would want to live there himself. Maybe Darcy's notion of taking a townhouse in London was not such a bad one after all.

Of course it was a good idea. It came from Darcy.

Did he have any idea how maddening it was when he was so often right? That would be something worth asking Liza about. No doubt she had devised a means of dealing with that most annoying trait.

Pleasing as that notion was, it must wait for another time. They had arrived at the solicitor's office, and there was a great deal to be accomplished.

Fitzwilliam stalked up the grand stairway, taking them two, even three. at a time. Darcy was bloody right, as bloody usual. Now, Fitzwilliam was not fit for company. Taking dinner on a tray in his chambers was a bloody good idea.

Halfway down the corridor, he paused at Miss Elliot's door. Perhaps they could converse through the closed door. That would not violate propriety, would it? He poised to knock, but a violent bout of coughing on the other side stayed his hand. Blasted, bloody hell—no one could converse with a cough like that plaguing them.

He stomped off to his own chambers, barely containing the urge to slam the door. That would only attract questions and attention—neither of which he had any desire for.

The only thing he desired was to share the intelligence of the day with the one person to whom it would actually matter. Granted, Liza would gladly listen to him. She always did. But it did not actually make any difference to her whether his drawing room would be large enough.

Gah!

He threw up his hands and paced along the fireplace. If he did not get some answers soon, he would surely run mad. Barking, bloody mad!

Knotting his fingers in his hair, he paused by the window.

Breathe, man, breathe.

Get a hold of yourself. You have spent the day running from ghosts, and it has driven you to the edge of Bedlam. You are stronger than this.

His heart slowed just a bit, but the racing prickles continued along his shoulders. Sitting still would only agitate him more.

Enough of this stupidity! He needed to communicate, so he would do just that.

He pulled out his desk chair with a thump and dropped into it. A letter was in order, so a letter he would write.

Propriety be damned.

Miss Elliot,

As you may know, I have visited Listingbrook for the first time. Darcy pronounced the farms and fields in fine condition. You may not be aware that, coming from him, those rather sedate words are in fact a great compliment. He suggests that everything looks in order to begin spring planting in due course. A few of the houses need some minor repairs, but nothing that cannot be accomplished with relative ease. However, I know, at least at the moment, none of that can be of great interest to you.

Darcy assures me that the reports of Listingbrook's income are in line with what he has seen, perhaps even slightly underestimated. Currently the estate provides two thousand five hundred pounds a year. Over the next ten years, Darcy believes it might be increased, with the purchase of several adjacent small farms, and some improved farming practices, to three, even four thousand a year.

My sell-out will provide some few hundred pounds a year more, but I cannot see that being of great consequence. I imagine, forgive my forwardness on the matter, that your dowry will be much the same matter, assuming of course your father is able to pay out a yearly sum.

Pray understand, I do not fancy debt, though I know it is quite fashionable and acceptable. I will require that we live within the means provided.

So then, my first question to you: Will this sort of income, that will have to be carefully administered if Darcy's plans of increase are to be realized, be tolerable to you?

Fitzwilliam threw his head back and grumbled under his breath. What an incredibly romantic sentiment. Surely this would go down among the most poetic of letters.

He pushed to his feet and stretched. The audacity of this notion—writing her a letter.

A proper lady did not accept a letter from a man to whom she was not engaged.

But if no one else knew, she just might—and that was why he was writing and must continue.

He lowered himself back down and dipped his pen.

If your answer is affirmative, then I must discuss with you the matter of the house itself.

It is a manor house, in the way of most country houses befitting an estate with the income I just described. Overall, it is in good repair, though, as is always the case, a few minor things might need attention.

The house itself is three floors, with attics above, though those are mainly used for storage. The servant's rooms, nursery, and some minor guest rooms take up the third floor...

Another bout of coughing ripped through her chest, and Elizabeth fell back onto the mound of pillows, dragging air into her tortured lungs. Somewhere, there was a cup of coltsfoot tea—yes, there on the bedside table, on the one side of the bed not yet enclosed by the bed curtains.

Lovely, cozy things, bed curtains.

She rolled to her side and reached for the cup, nearly knocking it off the table. Oh, this was tiresome! Bah, it tasted terrible, too, but then, what healing potion—save peppermint and ginger—did not? At least this one actually seemed to help.

How cruel that this cold would be of the lingering variety when she had much better ways to apply her time. Would Colonel Fitzwilliam think her toying with him because of it?

Then again, if he were so untrusting, perhaps that was important to know. It was not the kind of life she wanted to live; one with a suspicious man always looking over her shoulder. A little shudder snaked between her shoulders. No, that would not do at all.

A sharp rap came at her door, followed by an odd sliding, rustling sort of sound.

She pushed up on her elbows and looked toward the door.

What?

No, it could not … but yes? A folded paper on the floor. Had someone slid it under her door?

Loud footsteps faded off down the hall.

Fitzwilliam's.

Fluttering heartbeats tickled her lungs into more coughing, but she slid out of bed and wrapped her dressing gown around her as she padded to the door.

A generous fire warmed the room, but it was not nearly so warm as it was inside the bed curtains, under mounds of blankets and feather beds. Chills pricked her arms and legs. She scooped up the paper and dove back under the bed linens.

Blast and botheration, she should have brought a candle nearer as well.

Another trip into the chilly air for the candle, a bed jacket, another pair of socks, and a glass of hot water and sweet wine. That should be everything she could possibly need for some time.

Once she stopped coughing and rewarmed herself under the blankets, she held the paper up in the candlelight.

Miss Elliot,

The hand was strong and masculine, but she did not need to see even that to know the author.

He had written her a letter!

How utterly improper.

How utterly delightful.

Butterflies fluttered in her stomach, and her hand trembled with delight.

Was this how girls just out felt when the first handsome young men asked them to dance?

How ridiculous. How stupid.

Tears prickled her eyes.

It was just her cold. It should not matter at all that he would breach propriety to communicate with her now. What did it mean that he was so impatient he could not wait to have a proper conversation with her?

Hot trails coursed down her cheeks. Apparently, it meant a great deal.

She unfolded the page. Gracious, he had written a vast amount!

Visited Listingbrook … Darcy's approbation … good condition … income …

That was to be his income.

A tickle at the back of her throat threatened to become another wracking cough. She held her breath until it passed.

By many standards, the sum was quite generous. Certainly one might live comfortably on such a sum, especially if not encumbered by debt.

But it was not the income of a baronet.

Neither, though, was it the income of mere farmers. It was more than sister Mary could expect from Uppercross. And it was more than Anne and Wentworth could boast.

Perhaps it was petty to even think of that. But there it was, she did think of it, and it was important to her. Bad enough that both her younger sisters were already married. To establish herself for less than both of them would have been intolerable.

And it seemed that Fitzwilliam understood that. The younger son of a peer, he probably did.

She was used to living with economy now. There was quite a bit she could do with that sort of income—and quite a bit she could not.

She returned to the letter.

Visited the house … housekeeper says the kitchens are in good order and the pantry well stocked … eight bedrooms, with several more possible if other spaces were refit … a morning room, small and large dining room, two parlors … and—

She gasped and doubled over with more coughing.

—a drawing room large enough for a small ball!

A room large enough to properly entertain! She bit her knuckle, but her vision blurred and throat tightened.

To be able to do more than host card parties and tiny dinners! Proper parties, and even a ball?

Of course, the society of Highbury remained to be seen. It could be dreadful. It probably was.

What else did he say?

The style of the house … definitely older … furnishings not new … like Hartfield, well kept, but not fashionable …Sir Walter would probably not approve, drapes are serviceable, in good condition, but not stylish…

Had Father been on his tirade about draperies and paper hangings again?

She covered her eyes with her hand. What must they all think of her, after having heard that from him?

What did Fitzwilliam think? She peeked through her fingers.

So there you have it, Miss Elliot, the details as best as I can present them. I have, to my knowledge, neither overstated, nor understated anything. I want you to understand full well what you might expect from me.

The matter is now in your hands.

I cannot wait though for an answer, I must know your opinion as soon as possible what is your opinion. So, pray, do this for me:

If you find what I have presented agreeable and are willing to see the estate and have further discussions of our plans, then have your abigail send a maid to my room with a tray bearing buttered toast, spread with sugar, and a cup of black tea.

If what you have read here is unacceptable, I full well understand. Since there is nothing more I can offer you, it means an end to our acquaintance. If that is what you wish, have your abigail send a tray with a slice of well-burnt toast and a decanter of brandy.

Pray end my suspense soon. If I do not hear from you in some way, I will infer meaning from that as well.

RF

P.S. I will take no offense if you choose to burn this letter to preserve necessary propriety.

Toast? The man was asking for a message in *toast?*

She laughed until tears fell and she coughed too hard to breathe.

If he wanted toast, then he would have it.

Fitzwilliam paced the perimeter of his chambers, dodging the furniture as he went. Was it peculiar that he knew exactly how many paces would take him from one corner to the next, from one obstacle to the next?

Probably.

But it was maintaining his narrow grip on sanity, and for that reason, he would continue.

Would she respond to him? Would she even read his letter? It was so improper in the first place, and it was not as if the response he requested was conventional in any way, either.

Covert communications had never been his specialty in the army, and was not likely to become so now. But it was all he could think of that might not lead to suspicion if detected.

True enough, Liza would wonder why he wanted burnt toast, but no one would question the brandy.

A knock on the door.

He nearly jumped out of his boots and dashed for the door.

The poor maid trembled just a bit as she handed him a covered tray and ran off.

Was he really so frightful?

Probably.

He deposited the tray on his desk and stared at it, paced three circles around the desk and stared at it again.

The cover could not conceal a decanter—that should be good news, should it not?

Another knock?

The maid bore another tray, with a small, crystal decanter and glass.

His face turned cold as he took it from her, closing the door a little too loudly behind her.

So, now he knew.

He set the tray beside the other, poured himself a glass, and dropped into the somewhat lumpy chair by the fireplace.

At least she was kind enough not to play with him, increasing his suspense with coy—

This is not brandy!

His hands shook. Perhaps it meant nothing, but perhaps it meant everything, absolutely everything.

Two steps carried him to the desk. He threw off the cover.

Two slices of buttery sugared toast, and a cup of tea!

He barely set the glass down before spilling it.

Sugared toast.

He picked up the plate. A note!

A glass of rum will follow. I hope it is to your taste—your letter betrayed a shaking hand.

Bloody hell—she had a sense of humor!

He staggered back to the chair near the fire, toast in one hand, rum in the other.

Who knew they tasted so well together?

✾Chapter 6

ELIZABETH SNIFFLED AND DABBED her sore nose with a handkerchief. While her cold was the very reason she had the opportunity to stay here at Hartfield and explore a friendship with Colonel Fitzwilliam, it was difficult to be grateful for the sore throat, hacking cough, and stuffy nose.

Granted, her health was improving. Yesterday, she had managed to make it downstairs an hour before breakfast. She enjoyed the ladies' society in the parlor, even playing a little on the pianoforte for them. Unfortunately, Colonel Fitzwilliam had already left for the day, away addressing issues regarding Listingbrook. Mrs. Darcy suggested that his first visit had been a bit hesitant, but now he demonstrated an energy toward the place very similar to Mr. Darcy's.

Something about the way Mrs. Darcy held her head, or perhaps it was the lift of her lips and eyebrows. How much did she know? Surely Fitzwilliam would not have confided something so personal as his covert conversation with her. Would he?

No, he would not have. But Mrs. Darcy was curious.

The hair on the back of Elizabeth's neck prickled. Having someone interested in her affairs was always unsettling, even if it was benevolent. Lady Russell had always bordered on intolerable. Anne often made her feel the same way, especially now that she was married and oh-so-devoted to taking care of others—whether or not they wanted it.

Did she really need another sister like Anne? Not that Mrs. Darcy was actually sister to Colonel Fitzwilliam, but the relationship seemed close enough that an intimate connection with that family would be expected. Anne was a good soul, though, and did not hold a grudge against her, although the opportunity—and sufficient provocation—were there.

She had not been a very good sister to Anne—or to Mary for that matter. Especially after they had received offers of marriage, and she did not. Perhaps she should have learned something from that. Maybe if she had allowed herself to have been softened and touched by those experiences, she would not be approaching thirty—thirty! What a ghastly age to be—without ever having even a real suitor, much less an offer.

At least until now.

She sat up and swung her feet to the floor. The room spun a little, but the lightheadedness passed enough for her to reach for her dressing gown. With a little help from her maid, she should be presentable and ready to join the house party in short order. She rang the bell.

"Is this what you wish?" Her abigail adjusted the mirror so Elizabeth could see her hair.

"No, it is far too elaborate for the day time." She began to pull out the pins. "Where is my wool shawl?"

"Are you certain? It is not considered fashiona-ble—" she retrieved the shawl from the closet.

Elizabeth snatched up the shawl and wrapped it over her shoulders. "I am well aware of what is fash-ionable. That was never my question."

Having a cold was far less fashionable than any shawl might be.

"Bring up some tea." She dismissed the maid with a flick of her fingers. Perhaps when she returned, the girl might be of a better mind to do her hair properly.

Wan sunlight filtered through the sheer curtains, not enough to warm the room, but its presence made everything seem somehow warmer. Only the final traces of snow remained on the ground, lingering in the shadows. Somehow it all looked hopeful.

Rather like she felt at the moment. She twirled in place, clutching her shawl about her.

Now she was just being silly. Best she get dressed, even without her maid's help. If the gentlemen want-ed to eat early, she needed to be ready.

She slipped into her gown—not a frumpy morning gown, but something simple and pleasing, fitting for a morning at home.

Would Colonel Fitzwilliam join them for breakfast? It was so maddening not to have seen him since...

She looked over her shoulder. The edge of his letter barely peeked out from beneath the cover of her journal, securely tied with an ivory ribbon. Probably should put that in a drawer—

A dainty knock made her jump.

"It is Mrs. Darcy."

Elizabeth sighed. Mrs. Darcy had been so diligent in attending her whilst she had been sick, it was a bit ungrateful to sigh. But there was another's knock she would far rather have heard. "Come in."

"I hope you do not mind. I intercepted the maid on her way up. I was so happy to hear you are feeling better, I just had to come for a visit."

"I did not send my maid for a breakfast tray—how odd. But you are very welcome, Mrs. Darcy. A little company sounds quite pleasant right now."

While that much was true, it was not Mrs. Darcy's company she had hoped for.

"It seems that your maid has not finished her morning duties. Might I help you with those buttons and perhaps pin up your hair?"

Elizabeth blinked. "My buttons?"

Mrs. Darcy stepped behind her and started fastening buttons. "Forgive me if I am too familiar. It is something my sisters and I were often wont to do. We shared a single girl between us all and only then, when she was not needed by the housekeeper. It was often more practical to assist each other."

Elizabeth sat down at the dressing table, eyes prickling. "I have two younger sisters, but we never did such a thing."

It had been a long time, a very long time since she had shared any kind of intimacies with another woman.

Mrs. Darcy began brushing her hair. "I imagine a baronet's household is run rather differently to a simple country gentleman's."

"Different, perhaps, but I would not necessarily say better. The household ran very differently when my mother was alive."

"I am sorry you lost her. I can only imagine how difficult that must have been." difficult."

"It was so long ago, that it is challenging to even remember. After that we went to school. My youngest sister Mary married shortly afterward—to a man whom my middle sister, Anne, rejected." Elizabeth swallowed hard, her throat still raspy and sore.

"Unless one has experienced it, it is difficult to imagine the indignity of having one's youngest sister married before any of the older ones. But I suppose my mother courted that sort of luck by having all five girls out at once."

"Five sisters out at once? How did your family manage the expense?" Elizabeth bit her lip. "Forgive me if that is too personal a question."

"It is personal, but not unreasonable. The honest answer is that none of it was managed well. My mother is a well-meaning woman, but not a well-planning one. I believe that she intended to do more for us than she actually did. We attended assemblies and the occasional party in the neighborhood, and of course, she encouraged us to meet the militia officers."

"Your sister married one of them?"

"Yes."

Something in the tone of Mrs. Darcy's voice suggested there was far more to that story than a simple wedding. Something that she probably did not wish to discuss any more than Elizabeth wished to discuss Penelope and Mr. Elliot.

Yes, it was best to allow a few secrets, even among friends.

Mrs. Darcy tucked the last pins into her hair. "There now, certainly not what your maid might have accomplished, but serviceable enough for now. What do you think?"

"Perfect for this morning. Thank you." Elizabeth poured tea for them both.

Mrs. Darcy sat at the little table near the window, pulling her shawl a little more tightly around her shoulders. There was a bit of a draft, but the pretty view was worth it.

Elizabeth uncovered the breakfast tray and gasped.

Sugared toast and a tiny glass of something that was more than probably rum.

Mrs. Darcy laughed. "Upon my word! The only other person I have known who eats sugared toast in the morning is Fitzwilliam. What a remarkable coincidence."

"Indeed it is. I am … quite fond of it." Or at least she would be going forward, no matter what it tasted like.

Mrs. Darcy pursed her lips, a bit of a smile coming through. "No wonder your maid was in such a rush to get it to you. As I understand from Fitz, it is best eaten hot. Please, do go ahead."

Elizabeth nibbled at the edge. Sweet, crunchy, with a bit of cinnamon, too. It really was quite good.

Was it her maid's idea?

No, the girl would not dare be so cheeky. It had to have been him.

Whatever did he mean by it? Even if she did not know exactly, there was no doubt it was something good.

"It is good to see you looking so well. Fitzwilliam was so disappointed that you were unable to join us for dinner last night. He and Darcy arrived just before it was served, both so full of business that they could hardly talk of anything else. Perhaps if you had been there, they might have managed some polite conversation. But with only wives present, the gentlemen felt it entirely fair to talk of business all night. And can you guess where they are off to again today? I gather they are inspecting every handspan of the estate closely, and taking copious notes. My husband is nothing if not thorough." She laughed lightly.

No one would ever accuse Father of that. "How does the colonel find his new property? Have you seen it?"

"No, not yet. They have talked of inviting me along, but nothing more than that as of yet."

Elizabeth bit her lip. Was it wrong to be glad that Mrs. Darcy had not been there yet?

"I remember the first time I saw Pemberley, while traveling the district with my aunt and uncle. I learned a great deal about Mr. Darcy on that day, as we toured the house with his housekeeper. It is a pity that you shall have no such opportunity. Even when you see the house, it will tell you nothing about Fitzwilliam."

"You have known him a long time?"

"Almost as long as I have known Mr. Darcy." Mrs. Darcy sipped her tea and glanced out of the window, a faraway look in her eyes.

Elizabeth chewed her lip. Dare she? "Would you find it too forward of me to ask what you can tell me of him? We have so little time, and here in Highbury, we have no mutual acquaintances to help us come to know one another."

"You ask me to share his secrets?" Mrs. Darcy turned sharply and stared directly into Elizabeth's eyes.

Gracious!

"Certainly not, though, if there were something truly dark to him, I trust your character would not lead you to facilitate our acquaintance. You are his friend, and it seems that he and your husband are more like brothers than cousins. What can you tell me of his character? His likes, his dislikes?"

"He likes roast mutton, but detests liver. Do not serve it in the house at all, or he will leave until the smell has dissipated. When we visited Rosings at Easter, his aunt insisted liver be served. No sooner was the platter brought out than he stomped from the dining room and did not return until three days later, after having extracted a promise that there would be no more liver."

Elizabeth snickered. "I suppose then it is a good thing I am not a great fan of liver myself."

"Indeed it is. He also likes fish, but not shellfish. The texture, he says, is off-putting. He has an unfortunate taste for coffee in the morning, but strong black tea after that."

"That is all you know of him?"

"That is not enough?" Mrs. Darcy's eyebrow lifted in that maddening way she had.

Impertinent!

"I had hoped for more than what I might have

learned from his valet."

Now a wry smile. The woman was enjoying this far too much.

"Well said. Fitzwilliam is a complicated man, more so than many of his station. He has not enjoyed the privilege of the eldest, having to find a profession for himself in the army. Though it may be a gentlemanly profession, and he looks very smart with dashing uniform and sword, it has left a mark upon him. He does not speak of it, but there are times I can see a shadow upon his face. I cannot tell you more than that."

So it had not been her imagination. Mrs. Darcy had seen the same thing. What did it mean though? What darkness did he hide?

Mrs. Darcy took a sip of tea. "What I can tell you definitively is this: he is without a doubt the most loyal and faithful friend you can imagine. He would give anything in support of those he cares for. There is nothing with which I would not trust him, and I know that Mr. Darcy feels the same. I hope I am not being indiscreet in adding that I am quite certain that is a trait he deeply values as well."

The dark, piercing gaze Mrs. Darcy leveled upon her—the question was all too clear, more an accusation than an inquiry.

"I should take offense at that, madam. But I know that you care for him deeply and are considering only his welfare. You have nothing to fear from me. I have had too much of the intrigues of society and only wish for a quiet, peaceful existence now, much as he does. Or perhaps I am being too indiscreet myself?"

"Not at all, Miss Elliot." Mrs. Darcy nodded.

Why did the lady's approval leave her feeling warm and a little giddy?

"I have been called impertinent more than once in my life, but I have found there are times directness serves us quite well." Mrs. Darcy's eye twitched in a little wink. "And whilst I am being direct, I do so hope that you will be able to join us tonight. The entire house party has been invited to the Knightleys' friends, the Coles, tonight for a home theatrical and standing supper after. Mr. Woodhouse has declined the invitation, too many drafts, you know, and he suggests that it would be best if you did so as well. But there are those of us who would enjoy your company. What do you say?"

"I do not recall ever having been to a home theatrical. They are not something my father found appealing. But, I think I should like very much to attend."

Mrs. Darcy stood. "I am very glad to hear it. I shall let Mrs. Knightley know directly." With a nod, she left.

Given the look on Mrs. Darcy's face, Fitzwilliam was planning on attending. Perhaps they would be able to share some conversation tonight. That would be very pleasing.

It would be interesting to meet the local society— interesting and perhaps a little telling. She swallowed hard.

No, gloomy thoughts would not do for now. Better to enjoy her breakfast, join the company for the day, and try to sort out what would be best for her to wear on her first foray out into Highbury society and, more importantly, her first time to be in company with Fitzwilliam.

Darcy, Bennet, Knightley, and Fitzwilliam sat in the parlor, waiting upon the ladies—a full quarter of an hour now. A small decanter of port sat on the table between them whilst candlelight cast lively shadows along the walls.

A steady tick-tick-tick from the venerable -eight-day clock resounded through the room. Darcy kept his face turned away from the clock—rather obviously.

Tongue in cheek, Bennet laughed. "You need to relax, Darcy. It is still a quarter of an hour before we said we would leave. The ladies are not even late, yet. I fear you would never have weathered a household of five daughters. Pray that my daughter gives you sons, instead."

Darcy sniffed and looked away, a hint of color rising along his jaw.

He was such a stiff-rump. Though Liza had effected some changes in him, his sense of humor still needed work.

A great deal of it.

Bennet turned to Knightley. Good of him to give Darcy a moment or four to recover his equanimity. "Are home theatricals common in Highbury?"

"I would not say so. The aristocracy may find them all the kick, but they are beyond the reach of most of our modest community." Knightley leaned back and crossed his ankles.

"Then the Coles …?" Fitzwilliam asked, avoiding Darcy's penetrating gaze.

What was so wrong with wanting to know more about the people whom he was to meet?

"The Coles?" Knightley clucked his tongue and flashed his eyebrows. "Ah, the Coles. They are a good sort of family, but it has taken some time for Mrs. Knightley to accept them. They are in trade, though their fortune is quite respectable. They entertain a great deal and like to fancy themselves part of the local gentry."

"And the local gentry, I assume, politely does not correct their presumption?" Bennet said.

"I see you have the same sort of family near Longbourn as well?"

"We dine with four and twenty families, my wife would be quick to tell you." Bennet chuckled and shrugged.

"In any case, their manners are excellent, and they are good company. It is a small enough thing to ignore a little presumption now and again, especially when you consider the rather limited society that Highbury offers. You come from aristocratic connections, Fitzwilliam. Does your family indulge in amateur theatricals?" Knightley asked.

Darcy cringed.

Fitzwilliam snickered. "Indeed they do. My mother hates them, but my brothers and sisters find them an excellent tonic against boredom. Typically they perform several during the year. One of the large drawing rooms at the country seat has been given over to the endeavor."

"Do you act with family? Darcy, do you—"

"Hardly." Darcy snorted.

"I am surprised to hear that." Bennet flashed his eyebrows. "I thought surely Pemberley would be the seat of Derbyshire's finest entertainment."

"He does not perform to strangers. Ever." Fitzwilliam rolled his eyes. "I have assisted my siblings with a few minor parts, but on the whole, acting is not to my tastes. Will there be a large group there to-night?"

"I suppose it depends on what you consider large." Knightley glanced over his shoulder, through the doorway. "Ah, the ladies approach."

The gentlemen rose.

Fitzwilliam elbowed Darcy. "And with several minutes to spare. You do realize that no one is as utterly obsessed with time as you."

"And yet my wife tolerates me in spite of my foibles." Darcy cocked his head and tugged his shirt cuffs below his jacket sleeves.

If only he could be so lucky.

Fitzwilliam hung back and allowed the other men to proceed out of the door. Darcy was fortunate; his biggest foibles were being stodgy, rigid, and unsociable. On the whole, socially acceptable flaws. Of course, a good fortune made a great deal acceptable. He was not so lucky—either by his fortune, or his choice of flaws.

Perhaps this was a very bad idea all together. This evening, this endeavor, this connection with Miss Elliot—perhaps all of it—

"What are you doing, hiding back here?" Liza burst into the room, arms extended.

She paused a moment and caught his gaze. Her expression changed and that vaguely maternal look came over her. Two steps away, she stopped and balanced her hands on her hips, studying him in that way that felt far too much like a governess trying to discern what sort of mischief he had been up to.

"Not now, Liza."

"Yes, now. Precisely now." She glanced over her shoulder, caught Darcy's eyes, and waved for him to shut the door.

Instead of rescuing him, like a proper friend would have done, Darcy meekly closed the door, leaving him alone with her and the candlelight.

Gah!

"Tell me."

"There is nothing to tell." He looked aside. Her eyes were too much to bear. How did Darcy live with them? Always looking, always seeking to understand.

"Yes, there is. And if things are going the way I believe they are, you had best unlearn this little habit of lying about such things. I do not think that she will take to it any better than I do."

"You are overstepping yourself." He edged back a step.

"No, I am not. You would have stormed out if I were. I have seen you do it enough times. You want someone to crack through that ridiculous Fitzwilliam pride and reserve, but you do not want to admit it."

He grumbled deep in his throat.

"Thank you for agreeing." She stepped closer.

Too close.

Suffocatingly close.

"Since you are not choosing to be forthcoming, I shall offer you my theory."

"I do not want to hear your theory."

"Then tell me what is troubling you." She leaned a fraction closer. "You are feeling afraid … threatened?"

He stiffened and retreated.

Maddening, intrusive, insufferable woman!

"That is not the kind of thing you say to a man. Particularly to a military one."

"Of course, far be it from me to threaten your

manly vanity." She sighed and perched on the arm of a large wingback. "You are up to this, you know. You are entirely sufficient to this. You know how to be- have in company and are well-liked—far more than my husband. Darcy is impressed with your zeal and attention to your new estate—and you know that is a rare compliment from him. And as to Miss Elliot…." She left her perch and slowly approached.

It took all his determination not to retreat further.

"I think that she will be far more understanding than you expect. She has her own ghosts—not like yours to be sure—but her own, nevertheless. There is an odd commonality between you, of which I ap- prove very much. Do not throw that away easily." She slipped her hand in his arm and urged him toward the door. "It is time to leave, and there is a lady who would appreciate your escort."

He dragged his feet as he followed.

How did she do it? Such a tiny woman with the very force of a general behind her. She would have made a very good officer.

In the front hall, his valet helped him into his greatcoat. Miss Elliot stood nearby, adjusting her hood and tucking her hands into her muff. Neither Knightley nor his wife dressed as warmly, but after having been nearly stranded in weather so recently, neither she nor the Darcys were taking chances.

The night air was crisp, but not frigid. No smell of snow floated on the air. No clouds obscured the shimmering moon. An excellent night for an outing.

As promised, the trip to the Coles' was short and uneventful.

Fitzwilliam handed Miss Elliot out of the carriage

and offered her his arm on the way inside. "I am pleased you were able to attend tonight."

"Thank you. The boredom was becoming quite a trial. It feels like it has been quite some time since I have been able to be in company." She slipped her hand from her muff and tucked it in the crook of his elbow.

"I quite agree. It is certainly time to begin our conversations again—at least our conventional ones." He craned his neck.

Would she allow him to catch her eye?

Just a bit. Her eyes twinkled in the moonlight.

A warm, fuzzy knot grew in his chest.

Knightley waited for them at the door. "Mr. and Mrs. Cole, my I present my friends—"

Bows and curtseys and the appropriate level of fawning over Fitzwilliam's and Miss Elliot's connections. They were probably the highest-ranking guests that the Coles had ever hosted, given the expression Mrs. Cole wore.

Lovely.

He held his breath to restrain the sigh welling within. A fawning hostess. That did not bode well for the evening.

It could be worse, though. Focus on that.

Knightly ushered them into a brightly-lit parlor. Enough candles to light a ball, older furnishings, newly-upholstered, a few newer pieces, all fashionable. It could have been one of his mother's friends' parlors. The epitome of conspicuous consumption.

A dozen people milled about, speaking softly in small groups. The room went silent when they entered, and all eyes turned toward them.

"Knightley!" A woman in the far corner shrieked.

Mrs. Knightley sniffed and turned aside.

Interesting.

The loud woman, wearing an inappropriate ostrich plume, wove her way through the room, straight to them, a little like a peacock bearing down on a particularly succulent insect. A man who had the unmistakable carriage of a parson followed just a step behind.

"Knightley, you sly thing, you have been keeping guests and told us nothing of them!"

She tried to edge between Mr. and Mrs. Knightley.

Mrs. Knightley pressed closer to her husband.

"May I present Mrs. Elton and our vicar, Mr. Elton." Something in Knightley's voice sounded very, very patient.

It was not a good thing.

Was this an acquaintance Fitzwilliam wanted? Then again, if he were to live here, knowing the local vicar would be inescapable. He bowed from his shoulders as Knightley introduced him.

"A colonel! What stories you must have to tell. And an earl's son! How you distinguish our little company here—"

A bell, like one for servants, rang, and Mrs. Cole moved to the center of the room. "We are ready to begin, if you will follow me to the drawing room."

Reprieve!

Fitzwilliam offered his arm to Miss Elliot and fell in behind Darcy and Liza.

The drawing room was ample, but not huge, and clearly dedicated to the purpose. From the look, it was very intentionally done, no haphazard enterprise here. A short stage, maybe eighteen inches high, elevated the players for the audience. His brothers would be jealous. They had tried to convince Mother to allow them to install one at Matlock which she categorically refused.

The curtain across the stage was crafted of good quality fabric and dressed with a bit of fringe. The chairs, though, were not all matched. They were similar, but a close look revealed that they came from several differing dining rooms and possibly from the hallways throughout the house. So, some expense had been spared in the making of this production. All told, that was probably a good thing.

Mrs. Cole tried to usher him to the front of the chair-lined room. Fitzwilliam insisted he would rather sit near the back, muttering something about the army instilling the need to be ready for an emergency, so he would sit near a door. She finally relented.

What excuse had Miss Elliot offered to sit in the rear of the company as well? Something about still having a touch of a cough and not wishing to disturb the actors? In any case, it was utterly brilliant. He offered her as warm a smile as he dared.

"I am glad you approve," she whispered.

Her cheeks colored, just a bit, as she smiled. She was a pretty woman.

The rest of the guests seated themselves, that loud Elton woman prattling the entire time. The taste in furnishings, how very like that in Mr. Suckling's seat, Maple Grove, wherever and whatever that was. How had she devised to sit front and center? No doubt she thought very well of herself, indeed.

Mr. Cole stepped in front of the curtain and the room hushed. Naturally, Mrs. Elton's was the last voice to still.

Was it possible to dislike someone after only five

minutes' acquaintance?

"Thank you for joining us for our performance tonight. Without any further ado, I present our rendition of the Bard's '*Taming of the Shrew*.'" He scooted out of the way, and the curtain drew back.

At least they were sticking to a classic and not fumbling about with some modern atrocity as so many home theatricals were apt to do. As his brothers had tried to do.

Could they have chosen a more offensive work to present to Mother on her birthday? Best not to think on that right now.

Beside him, Miss Elliot sat very straight—straighter than even a proper young lady was apt to do. Her eyes were fixed on the stage.

Though he should have focused on the stage, he could not tear himself away from the drama beside him. She grimaced, gasped, bit her lip, and pressed a knuckle to her mouth. As multiple suitors vied for the hand of the fair younger sister, Bianca, she quivered and began to cough. But it bore little resemblance to the chest-wracking coughs that had seized her earlier in the day.

She jumped to her feet and excused herself from the room.

No doubt the theme of the play upset her—and knowing her situation, who could blame her?

She should not be alone, not at such a time.

He slipped out, and, with the help of a servant, found her in a small morning room lit only by the candlelight through the doorway from the adjacent rooms. "Do you need anything—tea with honey, perhaps, for your cough?"

She dabbed her cheek with her handkerchief. "No,

thank you. I am well. You need not miss the show on my behalf."

He stepped a little closer, standing just behind her shoulder. "You are not well at all."

"All the more reason for you to grant me a bit of privacy by which means I might preserve my dignity."

"Is that truly what you want?" He leaned down, nearly whispering in her ear. "If it is, I shall go. But somehow, I think not."

She gulped in one breath, then another, quivering just a little. "I am being foolish. There is no need to pay attention to it."

"Sensitive perhaps, but I can hardly call you foolish. I do not think anyone appreciates being reminded of things which are unpleasant."

She glanced over her shoulder and nearly bumped noses with him.

He shuffled back so fast that he nearly tripped over his own feet.

She pressed the back of her hand to her cheek. "It is unbecoming for one to shatter at the mere mention of disagreeable things."

"Some things are so powerful, that it is entirely understandable to shake apart when they come up." He set his jaw.

If she could not accept—

She wrapped her arms around her waist and squeezed her eyes shut. "You are very understanding."

"I have reasons for that."

"I suppose we both do." She peeked up at him.

Oh, the look in her eyes—so soft, so vulnerable. He leaned a little closer. "Come to Listingbrook with me—tomorrow perhaps? I very much want you to see the house and the grounds. We can go early in the morning, on horseback, before anyone else has arisen. That way there will be no expectation or pressure. If you do not like the house, I want you to be free to say so."

"Your description leaves me predisposed to think well of it." Her eyes shimmered, and she blinked hard.

"I cannot pretend to be displeased at that, but I must have your honest response. That is one thing I will absolutely demand from you. There is a great deal upon which I am willing to compromise, but I require honesty from my friends."

"I do not think that is too much to ask from one's friends."

He disengaged her hand from her waist and raised it to his lips. Perhaps he lingered in the kiss a mite too long, but it felt entirely right and proper. The glimmer in her eye suggested she agreed.

He offered his arm. "Are you up to returning to the theater? I should be interested to see how Katharina's final speech is interpreted. There are some, you know, who argue that she is entirely disingenuous in her speech and that Petruchio faces a most interesting life."

She slipped her hand into the crook of his arm. "And there are those who argue her change is genuine and of a most romantical nature, out of deepest love for him."

"Shall we see how this company plays it?"

"Indeed sir, let us proceed."

∾Chapter 7

JUST AFTER DAWN the next morning, Fitzwilliam
paced along the base of the great stairs, looking for all
the world like Darcy waiting for his female Fitzwilliam cousins to be ready for an event.

What a laugh Darcy would have, seeing him now.

But he must not. No one must know their errand.

To take Miss Elliot to Listingbrook alone was tan-
tamount to inviting her to be mistress of his estate
and announcing their engagement. Now was not the
time for such a thing. She needed the opportunity to
draw an honest, unencumbered opinion about the
house, for herself—and to share it with him. If she
was to accept what he had to offer, it had to be without pressure or fear of losing face.

She might insist that she could do that with a full
party visiting the house. But for him, visiting by

themselves was the only way he could be certain that he had her honest reactions.

A few minutes later, Miss Elliot appeared at the top of the stairs with her abigail, both in riding habits.

He probably should not smile so, but the expression was impossible to suppress.

A woman never looked better than while wearing a riding habit. The elegant cut and fit, the smart hats that went with them. The women could keep the ball gowns and opera dresses. He would gladly see his wife dressed daily in riding habits.

"Do you ride often?" he asked, meeting them at the base of the stairs.

"Not so much now we have established ourselves in Bath. But at Kellynch I rode daily." Her cheeks colored just enough to compliment the deep blue of her riding costume.

Had she any idea blue was his favorite shade?

"A morning ride is a favorite custom of mine. Shall we?" He led the way outside.

Two grooms held their horses ready near the mounting block. While the maid was a bit awkward in mounting her horse, Miss Elliot's easy grace implied an accomplished horsewoman.

Excellent news, indeed.

He pulled his horse alongside hers, and they rode in silence for a quarter-hour.

"How shall I know when we have crossed the boundary into Listingbrook?" she asked.

"There is a signpost at the crossroads that marks the southern boundary of the estate. It is quite a pretty approach to the house all told, through a stand of hardwoods, with a flower garden to one side and a wilderness to the other. Behind the house are ample kitchen gardens—or at least the housekeeper assures me they are. Gardeners remain on staff, so there will be no interruption in the supply from the gardens."

Another quarter-hour's silence followed.

This did not bode well. Perhaps she was anxious. But still, to be unable to hold even a light conversation? Perhaps with a subject less challenging.

"What did you think of the denizens of Highbury? I am convinced the Coles invited everyone of quality in the village." He forced his voice to remain light.

"Everyone and then some." A little wry smile crept up her lips.

Finally!

"It seems you have someone in mind?"

"And you do not? It seemed you formed some rather decided opinions of the vicar's wife." She cocked her head at him, her eyebrow lifted as though she knew his thoughts.

A little like Liza.

"Gah!" He glanced away and smacked his lips. "I would not say she is even an acquired taste."

"Whatever do you mean? She is ever so helpful to one and all in the parish. Or could you not detect the excessive gratitude that is directed toward her from all whom we met last night?"

He snickered. "Remind me not to get on your wrong side, Miss Elliot, for I fear your opinions are as pointed as my sword."

"And yours are ever so gentle, of course. It was quite clear that you will be hoping Mrs. Knightley invites her to tea this very afternoon, as she threatened to do just before we departed last night."

"Then I may be forced to give up the beverage entirely and keep to coffee for the rest of my life."

"Mrs. Darcy considers coffee an unfortunate habit, you know."

"She mentioned she finds my preference for morning coffee crude and unrefined, an opinion she no doubt holds of the Elton woman as well," he said.

"Did you notice how Mrs. Churchill seemed to avoid her?"

"Rather like one avoids a mad dog, I would say."

Miss Elliot covered her mouth to hide—not very well—a smirk. "I wonder what kind of bite she suffered."

"Are you suggesting the vicar's wife needs a muzzle?"

She gasped and pressed a hand to her chest. "I never said such a thing. Do not put words in my mouth."

"I might have put words in your mouth, but I did not place the thought in your head. That was entirely your own doing."

"I would submit that a guilty conscience sees in others what he himself is guilty of." She cocked her head just so.

That expression, in a riding habit, on a horse, in the English countryside … this might require a bit more self-control than he had anticipated. Perhaps it was good that the maid had come along after all.

Had Elizabeth any idea what he was thinking?

It was difficult to tell. For all the years she had been in the marriage mart, it did not seem that anyone had ever shown a great deal of interest—save that cad Elliot, of course. Perhaps she lacked the wiles possessed by so many of her peers, particularly the awareness that she was uncommonly attractive.

How good it was to hear him laugh. There had been so little humor at Kellynch. She had only recently discovered the pleasure to be had in it. He seemed no stranger to the indulgence.

It was a little too easy, though. The local society was so ripe for comedy. Mrs. Elton was a more parody than a person. Then there was Miss Bates whose sincerity and affectionate nature saved her from being utterly pathetic. Still though, she *was* utterly pathetic. Frank Churchill, even with the steady, moderating influence of his sweet wife, was still just shy of being a dandy—or a fop—she had not yet decided. Either way, it was clear that none of the men of sense gave him much credit, though they did seem to be trying to take him under their wings. Perhaps it was out of respect for his father, Mr. Weston. that caused that. Still, there seemed little enough harm in him.

Colonel Fitzwilliam pointed at the signpost. One arm extended just to the left with "Listingbrook" neatly painted in white letters.

She swallowed hard. Soon, she would be called upon to make probably the most important decision of her life. Pray let it be a clear and obvious one.

He turned down the left hand road and she followed, holding her breath. He did not look at her.

Was he as nervous as she? Something in the way his horse shook its head suggested that he was.

Odd, how it made it all just a mite easier to think that she was not the only one suffering so.

As promised, old hardwoods shaded the road. Their branches arched upward, over the road, almost intertwining above them. It felt stately, even a little protective. Certainly neat and well-maintained.

Beyond, she could make out stands of old growth woods—a sign of wealth and properly- maintained lands. Her father would scoff, but then he had shown his lack of proficiency at management at Kellynch, where few such stands remained.

The promised flower garden was enclosed by a low brick wall, gravel paths weaving between the beds. A few heathers, her favorite flower, still bloomed, somehow undaunted by the recent snows.

The sight should not bring tears to her eyes.

But it did.

Silly woman! Now was not the time for sentimentality. Practical. It was time to be practical.

The house rose up before them, just as Fitzwilliam had described it. Three storeys, plus attics. A stone elevation, with ample windows, and gables. There must have been an addition made to the west wing at some point. Some of the angles did not match correctly, and there was something just a little different about the styling of the windows.

Father would find fault with it. At one time, she might have as well. But that was another time and another woman. Now, now it felt quaint and rather inviting. A little like a crooked smile from an old friend.

A man met them at the front to take their horses—a groom or a gardener, perhaps? Still, it spoke well of the housekeeper that she had them attended to immediately.

Fitzwilliam waited for her at the door, tugging his jacket and fussing with his shirt cuffs. "Shall we? Into the abyss, as they say."

It could not be that bad, could it?

He opened the door, and she followed him in.

"Mrs. Amhurst." He nodded at a sturdy woman in a drab gown, mobcap, and apron. The housekeeper, no doubt.

She curtsied, one eye on Elizabeth. No doubt she suspected what was about.

And she would talk. Servants always did. They would have very little time before rumors abounded, and some kind of announcement would have to be made.

There was little helping it, but still …

"We will show ourselves about and seek you later with any questions." He dismissed the housekeeper with a curt nod, and she scurried away. "So where would you like to begin?"

Somewhere practical; the kitchen or the mistress's office, or perhaps the attics. That would be the correct answer. It would be useful to see what was in storage there.

"What about the large drawing room? You might consider how it would accommodate a ball?" His eye twitched in a wink.

Was it just an idle tease that caused him to suggest that, or did he suspect something more? They had never talked much about balls … or had they?

Had he inferred so much from such little conversation? Heavens! If he did—no one had ever paid that much attention to what she said. Ever.

He led her past the main stairs, toward the back of the house, stopping at an ornately carved door. Excellent workmanship, unique design. A little dust nestled into the deeper crevices of the carvings. It could do with a proper cleaning and polishing. But that was easily remedied. If a widower had lived here before, then he might not have used the room often enough to notice.

Fitzwilliam swung the door open. Sunbeams poured through the doorway. Someone had opened the curtains ahead of their visit.

He ushered her in ahead of him, and she peeked in.

Large windows, flanked by heavy draperies, filled the room with light. Not new enough to be fashionable, but the drapes were of good quality and well-maintained. Couches, settees, chairs, a pianoforte opposite the fireplace. Landscape paintings on the walls with a curiosity cabinet and shelf of books opposite the windows. Furniture moved aside, the room would accommodate twenty couples dancing, perhaps one more or one fewer. Certainly sufficient to have a ball in this neighborhood.

That should not be so important. It would not be so to a woman like Mrs. Darcy.

She pressed her fist to her lips. How mortifying! Mrs. Elton would probably understand her feelings, especially since a parsonage would not accommodate a ball.

"You approve?" he whispered, the barest tremor in his voice.

"Very much."

He released a deep breath and pulled his shoulders back a little straighter. Some of his tension seemed to slough away. "Come then, let me take you to the parlor on the other side of the house. It is not nearly so grand as this room, but I think it quite adequate for daily use."

His steps were so light he might well have skipped to the parlor. He flung open a painted door. "What do you think of—"

An odd popping noise cut him off. His eyes grew wide and a little wild, He ducked into the parlor, casting about from one window to the next, searching for something.

She bit her lip. Why was he behaving so strangely?

Dare she ask, or would that further agitate him?

After a few minutes, he settled a bit and straightened his coat. "Excuse my distraction, please. I think you will find this room quite cozy—"

A rifle report and then another rang out.

"Get down!" He launched himself at her, knocking her to the floor and covering her body with his. "Keep your head down!"

What was he doing? Had he gone mad?

She struggled against him, no match for his strength.

"Don't move. That's an order. Stay quiet. They will pass." He pressed her head down until her cheek lay on the faded carpet.

Did the gunfire have him believing that he was suddenly in the army once again?

What did he think he was doing? How dare he handle her person in such a way?

His hard, angular form weighed down upon her until she could barely breathe. Why was he—doing this?

Another shot cracked in the distance. He wrapped himself a little more firmly around her.

Heavens above! He was protecting her!

"Oh, Colonel, sir!" the housekeeper gasped from the door way. "Pray forgive me for not telling you.

Mr. Markham deputized Mr. Barnes of the next estate over to hunt on this land. I clean forgot to warn you of the hunting party, sir."

Fitzwilliam rolled to his side, his weight now off Elizabeth, and slowly pushed himself to his feet. He stomped toward the housekeeper. "Never, never forget to tell me of such a thing in the future. Do I make myself clear?"

"Very clear, sir." The housekeeper curtsied and backed away.

Elizabeth rose, slowly, carefully, watching him as she did.

He turned his back to her, not even offering her assistance to stand.

With a sharp grunt, he stormed from the room, without as much as a backward glance.

Fitzwilliam nearly collided with the housekeeper in the front hall.

"Is there something wrong, sir?" A familiar expression of fear darkened her eyes.

How many times had he seen that look? He probably deserved it, but it did not make things any better knowing it.

It made them worse.

"No, nothing. See to Miss Elliot. Take her on a tour of the house and anything else she wishes to see. Answer her questions, keep nothing back."

"Will you be returning, sir? Shall I prepare breakfast or tea?"

"No, I will not be returning. Prepare anything Miss Elliot wants." He pushed past her and flung the front door open.

Air. Cool, crisp air.

Damn and bloody hell! Traces of gunpowder on the breeze.

Damn hunters.

Damn deputization.

Damn Markham.

Damn everything.

He broke into a jog toward the stable.

That helped.

Sweaty and breathless, he grunted at the groom who had his horse ready in very short order.

The same dark, questioning fear was in his eyes.

Damn.

He mounted and took off, urging the horse into a trot. If only they could run all the way back to London and forget that this place ever existed or that any of this had ever happened.

But he could not.

He could not forget her.

But they had not known each other very long. He should focus on that.

Not her sense of humor. Her efficient practicality. Her sharp wit. Her excellent manners. Her understanding of society. Her intriguing conversation. Her excellent figure.

The way she looked in a riding habit.

Why did she have to look so bloody good in a riding habit? Anything else, he could have ignored—possibly with some effort—but he could have ignored it. But that?

There was no doubt, Providence was entirely against him.

What else could explain inheriting an estate and meeting a compatible woman, only to have it end like this?

But was it an end?

Of course it was. What else could it be?

He had shown himself in the most clear, unmistakable way. He was broken. A fool. A coward, half-mad with remembrances and tempers and ghosts that chased him in the night.

After being thrown bodily to the ground with him forcing her to remain there—what must she think of him after such an assault?

She had said nothing—but what could she have said? The way she looked at him …

How had she looked at him?

Had he even noticed?

It did not matter. She would have looked at him with fear or pity—either was nigh on intolerable.

And she would want nothing to do with him now that she knew.

He did not blame her. He would feel the same. At least she had the opportunity to know before he made an offer.

Thank Providence that she and her maid could return separately to Hartfield, with none the wiser. There was something to be thankful for.

He rode the perimeter of Listingbrook before he turned back for Hartfield. That would give her plenty of time to return, for her outing to appear utterly unconnected with his. Even if someone suspected, no one of their party wished to see either of them forced into marriage. They would be discreet. It would be well.

Somehow, it would be well.

He handed his horse off to a groom. Poor creature deserved some proper attention and a good cool down. He had probably ridden it too hard.

Of course, add one more sin to the list today.

Just inside the door, the housekeeper intercepted him. "Excuse me, sir. Mrs. Knightley has guests to tea. She asked that you join them when you return."

Tea and company? What could possibly be worse?

Insulting a hostess who had gone beyond all expectations to be gracious and accommodating.

Much as he would rather do otherwise, it simply could not be ignored. Contrary to his mother's opinion, she had instilled in him some manners. Mrs. Knightley had done too much for him to warrant anything but the greatest of courtesy.

Tea and company it would be.

"They are in the small drawing room, sir."

He nodded, handed her his coat, and straightened his jacket. Polite behavior for an hour would not kill him.

Probably.

Soft, conversational voices wafted into the corridor. Knightley and Darcy were there with two other men he had met at the Coles'. The women's voices all blended together in a birdlike hum. Usually Liza's stood out—was she biting her tongue for some reason?

He peeked into the small drawing room, by far the most feminine room in the house— and the most fashionable. Had Mrs. Knightley had it redone recently?

"Colonel Fitzwilliam," Mrs. Knightley rose from the settee near the window and set aside her sewing.

"I am so very pleased that you have arrived in time to join us."

"Do join us." Knightley beckoned him toward the knot of men in a cluster of wingbacks near the unlit fireplace.

Darcy, and was that Weston? And the vicar?

"Colonel!"

And the vicar's horrid wife.

Providence indeed hated him.

At least Miss Elliot was not among them.

"The poor man has barely come off his horse. Give him a little time with his own kind before you drag him into your matronly circle." Knightley laughed, but his eyes betrayed him. He was not joking, and it would be best for all involved if Mrs. Elton did not try to argue with him.

Imagine that. She smiled and returned to her previous conversation. How many rather direct encounters had she had with Knightley to engender such capitulation?

If he stayed in the neighborhood, he would have to ask.

But he would not. Tomorrow he would see the solicitor and set about leasing out Listingbrook.

"Returning to your old habits, I see—out at dawn, on horseback." Darcy cocked his head, his eyes asking far more than his words.

"There are many pleasant vistas in the area," Weston said. "You should join us for a shooting party—"

Fitzwilliam jerked back. Bloody hell and damnation!

"You do not want to invite Fitzwilliam shooting. I make it a point never to do so, myself." Darcy shook his head, carefully avoiding Fitzwilliam's gaze.

"Really? Why would that be?" Elton's brows twitched, and he gave Fitzwilliam a sideward glance.

Zounds! What was that ninny thinking?

"Having trained far too many men to count in the art of shooting, he is a crack shot. Not only will you go home empty-handed, but your pride will be worse for the wear. No, if you want sport with him, fishing would be the thing. There he has no advantage, unless he has learned to speak to the fish themselves since I last went with him."

Weston laughed. "I appreciate the warning. Fishing it is then, though it will have to wait for spring."

Fitzwilliam eased back a bit into the wingback. "I will hold you to that. What runs in your streams here? There is a bit of a pond on Listingbrook."

"Markham kept it stocked with … well, blast it all now, I cannot recall what—perhaps salmon—but the fish were fat and excellent fried up in the late spring and early summer."

"That sounds like a request for an invitation to me." Knightley winked.

"One I hope to be able to honor—"

"Miss Elliot!" Mrs. Knightley rose and hurried toward the door.

Miss Elliot paused in the doorway, still clad in her habit and gloves. Her riding hat was tipped ever so slightly to the right, just tempting a man to come by and straighten it.

She swept the room with her gaze, pausing to meet his eyes briefly. Her expression was entirely—what did one call such a look? Unaffected, unperturbed, neutral? It was as if nothing had ever happened.

She was an excellent actress and very kind.

The housekeeper peeked in, just behind Miss Elliot.

"Bring in the tea." Mrs. Knightley nodded at the
housekeeper and took Miss Elliot by the hands. "I am
so glad you could join us!"

She walked Miss Elliot back to the group of ladies.

Elton and Weston yammered some sort of fish
story. He attempted to nod and grunt in the correct
places, but with her sitting there, just in a sunbeam,
how could he possibly pay attention? Her profile was
stunning, her posture perfect.

Damn.

Why did she have to show that off now that everything had turned entirely arsey-varsey?

Darcy studied him, discreetly, but still, he
squirmed under the penetrating gaze. Darcy glanced
at Miss Elliot and raised an eyebrow.

Fitzwilliam turned aside.

Bloody hell, would he not simply leave well
enough alone? It was not as if he would not know the
full story soon enough, but pray give a man a little
privacy.

The housekeeper and a maid bustled in with a
generous tea service: tea, sandwiches, fragrant baked
things, even a tureen of some sort of soup. His stomach grumbled.

He never had breakfast. Bless Mrs. Knightley's
generosity in setting her tea table.

"Would you gentlemen like to join us?" Mrs.
Knightley gestured them toward the elegantly arrayed
tea table.

Was it the match-making machinations of Mrs.
Knightley, or just the hand of Providence against him

once again that had him seated between Miss Elliot and Mrs. Elton?

Of all times, now would have been the proper moment for Liza to notice his dilemma and come to his rescue.

Naturally, she did not.

"I am pleased to see you feeling well enough to ride, Miss Elliot." Mrs. Knightley handed her a steaming cup of tea.

"Riding? I prefer driving the phaeton—you know, Mr. E. has placed one at my disposal. In fact we drove it here."

Fitzwilliam bit his lip. The image of Mrs. Elton driving while her husband rode beside her—

Miss Elliot coughed, but it sounded exactly like the expression she used to cover a snicker. Of course, she would find humor in that, too.

"Mr. Darcy is teaching me to drive and ride."

"And how do you like it? I am sure you find driving quite invigorating." That smug little smile Mrs. Elton wore—Liza would not tolerate it long.

Liza shrugged. "The freedom it affords is quite pleasing, but as he is also teaching me to ride, I would have to say that I much prefer riding."

Given the look on Darcy's face, he might just share Fitzwilliam's preference for a riding habit. No wonder he was teaching her to ride.

"Well, I am afraid that I neither drive, nor ride, but the countryside is still quite lovely on foot." Mrs. Weston nibbled on a dainty sandwich.

"It is some very lovely country. There are so many hardwood stands—such lovely avenues they create." Miss Elliot gave him the briefest of sidelong glances. "I could ride them for hours, I am sure."

"I do believe we have some of the best vistas between London and Box Hill." Mr. Weston leaned back in his chair, quite satisfied with his opinion.

"I have heard Box Hill is but seven miles away. Perhaps we might take in the views while we are here?" Liza said.

"I am certain we can arrange a party to go. The weather has quite turned, and it seems warm enough for a picnic." Mrs. Knightley glanced at her husband with the oddest expression.

"That could be arranged. But pray, let it be a larger party, with all of the gentlemen included." Knightley leaned forward, elbows on his knees. "We have had a bit of a problem with gypsies recently, and it would not do to send the ladies out on their own."

"Gypsies!" Mrs. Elton clutched her breast. "Mr. E., you had not told me! They are such entirely despicable creatures. I am quite in horror of them. You should have told me—you should have told me. I will not feel safe in my own home now. We must have a man to walk the house at night. Surely you must agree with me, Mrs. Weston?"

"While there can be problems with them, perhaps you are overreacting just a mite? I can hardly imagine them—"

"Certainly, you must refrain from riding out alone, Miss Elliot. It is not safe at all. Pray tell me you will not do so." Mrs. Elton leaned across Fitzwilliam and stared into Miss Elliot's face.

Miss Elliot avoided Mrs. Elton and gazed directly into Fitzwilliam's eyes. She spoke slowly, emphasizing each word. "I thank you for your concern, but I have never felt safer or more protected anywhere in my life—even on my father's estate. It is almost as if I have a guardian watching over me."

Fitzwilliam's eyes widened, and he swallowed hard.

She blinked slowly, lips curving up just a bit.

Mrs. Elton babbled something, and Liza interrupted, steering the conversation in an entirely different direction.

Liza was a treasure.

Protected. Miss Elliot felt protected. She could not possibly mean—

She turned aside to attend a question from Mr. Weston.

He tried to sip his tea, but his throat was too tight to swallow. And blast it all, his hands shook, nearly loud enough to rattle the tea cup and saucer. He set them on the table.

"Have you settled on a date to take possession of Listingbrook?" Mrs. Weston asked.

"I do hope it is soon. I so look forward to having another well-connected soul in the neighborhood. Increasing one's connections with other good connections is always most agreeable. Do you not agree, Mr. E?"

Fitzwilliam stammered a non-answer and allowed Darcy to fill in other equally useless information.

"Who will be keeping house for you? Will you be bringing a sister, a cousin, or an aunt, perhaps? I should like to host a little party to welcome her into our little community." Mrs. Elton folded her hands in her lap—a pose she must have learnt from a fashion plate—stiff, formal, and empty.

"I do not have any convenient relations to keep house for me." He struggled to avoid Mrs. Elton's gaze.

"We cannot have that! I know! We must see you married, Colonel. We simply must. But never fear; leave it all to me. I shall arrange to make introductions for you—I have connections all over the country."

Knightley grumbled under his breath.

"I thank you, but no, Mrs. Elton. I have no need—"

"Nonsense, it is not trouble at all, I assure you. I am entirely qualified to see to finding you the most eligible young ladies for introduction."

"I am not in need of introductions."

"Of course you are. How else will you find a wife? I will write to my sister, Mrs. Suckling, immediately."

"Pray do not. I do not want—"

"Do not be so brave about it all, Colonel. Of course you do. Mark my words. We will see you married by summer."

Fitzwilliam sprang to his feet, nearly upsetting the table. "No! No introductions. I do not need your help. I have already been introduced to the woman I want to marry."

Liza jumped up. "Mrs. Knightley, I think we are very much in need of some entertainment just now. Shall we perhaps adjourn to the music room?"

Darcy and Knightley hurried to Mrs. Weston and Mrs. Elton, escorting them out before Mrs. Elton could comment. They moved very, very quickly.

The door clicked shut.

Miss Elliot sat exactly where she had before, unaffected and staring out the window. Surely she must have been aware of his eyes on her. Her color was high, but her face serene. Had she not heard his hasty words?

He dodged around the chairs to stand before her. "Did you mean what you said?"

She rose, like Venus rising up from the waters. "I have never felt so safe and protected in my life."

"I was foolish and improper."

"And yet your first instinct was…" her voice cracked, "… was to ensure that I would be safe."

"From a threat that did not exist."

"It was real in your mind. How much more real need it be?"

"I must have frightened you. I could have hurt you."

"I was confused, for a moment." She shrugged.

"You have now seen me for what I am. Flawed. Broken. I will not do for you."

"You are not the one to judge that. We are all imperfect, are we not? Should I not determine what imperfections I am willing to live with?"

"I do not want your pity."

"And I do not want yours. I have been on the shelf, a spinster for so many years that I have lost count. I am old and unwanted, and for all my connections to title, I have very little to offer. You are not the only one who might be pitiable here."

"The war has left me a different man, plagued by memories and haunted by ghosts. Even my family tires of my presence. Liza and Darcy alone have been able to find the endurance to stand with me."

"Then I shall have someone to turn to for help." She smiled matter-of-factly.

"Do not make less of it that it is."

"Do not underestimate me." Oh, the fire in her eyes.

"It would be a very great mistake to underestimate you."

"It would be very good for you to remember that." She cocked her head just so.

He cupped her cheek with his palm. She pressed into his hand, eyes closed.

"Miss Elliot, you have one last chance to dash from this room and announce to the house party that you cannot imagine what they were doing leaving you alone with a mad old soldier."

"And if I do not?"

Slowly, very slowly, he leaned down and pressed his lips to hers, slipping an arm about her waist.

She melted into his embrace, meeting him with an unexpected passion.

"I believe, sir, that I have been compromised," she whispered, brushing her lips ever so lightly against his ear.

Control. He must restrain himself.

He pulled back to look in her eyes.

Teasing minx. She knew exactly what she was doing.

"Then, Miss Elliot, there is only one remedy for it. You will be my wife."

"What, no poetic declaration? Not even a question?"

"Do you really need it?" He leaned a little closer, resting his forehead on hers.

"Not unless you need more answer than this." She kissed him, eagerly, fervently.

How could he fail to respond in kind?

Hinges squealed.

He opened one eye.

"So, are we to wish you joy?" Given Liza's smile, she well knew the answer.

He laced his fingers with Miss Elliot's.

She squeezed his hand hard. "Yes, Mrs. Darcy, great joy."

Mrs. Darcy squealed like a little girl and pounced on them. It really was quite sweet, in a very familiar sort of way. Familiar was ... nice ... quite nice. Elizabeth swallowed back a lump in her throat.

Mrs. Darcy grabbed their hands and escorted—more like dragged to be entirely forthright—them to the sunny music room, where they were ambushed by well-wishers. The men, now including Mr. Bennet and Mr. Woodhouse, gathered around Colonel Fitzwilliam, slapping him on the back. The ladies gathered around her, led by a positively predatory-looking Mrs. Elton.

She needed a leash, like a lady's pug.

And a muzzle.

"Oh, you devious creature! You gave no sign, no sign at all. How were we to know that you and he had an understanding?" Mrs. Elton slipped her arm in Elizabeth's and pulled her in close. "You must know I would never have suggested ... if I had but known ... really, what were you thinking by keeping secrets from me?"

The cloying, sweet voice and the wide, batting eyes—gah! How might she have known—yes indeed, how might she have known?

Perhaps simply opening her eyes to someone other than herself?

Was it pure coincidence that Elizabeth and Fitzwilliam sat together at the Coles' theatrical, or that they were always in each other's company during the standing supper afterwards? Perhaps the furtive glances between Mrs. Darcy and Mrs. Knightley cast in their direction constantly during tea might have given some slight indication.

Truly, how self-absorbed and inattentive could one woman be—particularly one who considered herself at the apex of the local social circles?

Helping her to learn her proper place in society would not be a pleasant task, but considering the expression on Mrs. Knightley's face, it might be one Elizabeth could find herself ready help with.

Mrs. Darcy glared at Mrs. Elton. Too bad she did not live nearer. With Mrs. Darcy and Mrs. Knightley together, Mrs. Elton would have little choice but to recognize that she was not all she thought she was.

"We wish you joy, very great joy," Mrs. Darcy said a touch too firmly to just be kind words. If she hinted any more strongly at Mrs. Elton, one might accuse her of unladylike bluntness.

Not that Elizabeth would, of course, but someone else might.

Woe to them if they did.

"Of course we do, of course. Very great joy. What of the wedding, though?" Mrs. Elton dragged her to the faded sofa and sat far too close. "Where will you be married from?"

That was, unfortunately, a very good question. A sunbeam bore down upon the back of her neck, a trickle of sweat forming along her spine.

Kellynch, with the Crofts in residence, was out of the question. They might claim to welcome her, but there were too many difficult memories associated with that house.

Camden Place was a possibility. But then a wedding breakfast would be arranged to show them off to all Father's connections and supposed connections. Some dreadful gossip writer would surely attend—

A tall, comforting presence loomed over her with a heavy hand on her shoulder.

How improper—and protective—and utterly satisfying, especially when Mrs. Elton stared at his hand, jaw agape.

"If I might be so bold as to suggest, Hartfield would be a very fine place to be married from, if, of course, we might impose once again on our hostess." Fitzwilliam squeezed her shoulder just enough to ask if he had overstepped.

She laid her hand over his and patted the back of his hand with her fingertips. "What a very agreeable thought."

"Does that mean you would allow Mrs. Darcy and me to arrange a wedding breakfast on your behalf?" Mrs. Knightley smiled like a little girl.

"You must leave all the arrangements to me. You know that is my talent, arranging things of this sort." Mrs. Elton clapped softly. "I can see the table in my mind's eye, with hot house flowers—"

"No." Fitzwilliam's word hung in the air somewhere over Mrs. Elton's head, shadowing her face and leaving her gasping for words.

"You cannot mean that, Colonel, surely you cannot. Rest assured, every event I plan is the talk of Highbury—"

No doubt it was, but probably not for the reason she thought.

"I appreciate your offer very much, but it would be our privilege to make the arrangements for our cousin and his bride." Mrs. Darcy's face tightened into a patient, pleasant mask—an expression Elizabeth hoped never to be the recipient of. "I am aware of their favorite foods. Surely that should count for something." She winked.

No doubt a platter of sugared toast with cinnamon would appear on the breakfast table.

"You cannot be serious! Tell them, Mrs. Knightley!" Mrs. Elton's voice rose to nearly a shriek.

"Perhaps you might be useful to the new bride in other ways." Mrs. Knightley's lips stretched very tightly. She was probably containing a laugh given the sparkle in her eyes, even if there was a touch of desperation around the edges. "There must be someone to host the first tea and dinner in the couple's honor. For a couple of their standing, even a ball would not be inappropriate."

"A ball?" Mrs. Elton said the word slowing, trying it on for a fit like a new gown. "A ball—yes, that would be quite the thing! Leave everything to me! Mrs. Weston, will you not take the opportunity to assist me with the event?"

Mrs. Weston stammered something as she glanced from Mrs. Elton to Mrs. Knightley. The latter pleaded with her eyes.

"I think a ball is a lovely notion." Mrs. Weston's shoulders drooped slightly.

Mrs. Elton rose and paced from the pianoforte to the fireplace and back. "We shall have it at the Crown Inn—"

At least she did not want to hold it at that dreadful Ram's Horn. Elizabeth glanced up into Fitzwilliam's twinkling eyes. He must have had the same thought.

That was an expression she could become very accustomed to seeing.

Chapter 8

THE NEXT DAY Fitzwilliam rode out, Darcy in his shadow. With marriage settlements to hammer out, it probably was a good thing to have a second with him. If nothing else, it would prevent him from doing bodily injury to the arrogant baronet—or his own father if he became stubborn. Father had not been ungenerous with his other siblings, but he also had a hand in arranging their marriages.

Fate smiled on their errand, not once, but twice. First, they found the Lady Dalrymple and the Honorable Miss Carteret still in residence at the Dower House of the Viscount Dalrymple's estate and Sir Walter Elliot with them. Second and more importantly, Miss Carteret proved deeply interested in the business that had brought them.

When the baronet puffed his chest and questioned Fitzwilliam's suitability for his daughter, Miss Carteret pleaded his cause. Darcy did as well, but his case was not nearly so compelling as a pair of big brown eyes with impossibly long eye lashes batting over them. Sir Walter could little resist her insistence that there was no man more suitable for his daughter in all of England.

Darcy thought her interference more self-interest than anything else. Having Elliot's daughter out of the way would make a union with the baronet far more agreeable. But what did her motives matter as long as she was an ally?

Then the solicitors were brought in for the drafting of the settlement papers. Darcy's experience and acumen proved invaluable in drafting the papers, but once again it was Miss Carteret's influence that brought the affair to an agreeable close. She reminded Sir Walter that the details of the settlement would by no means remain private and that his reputation might be colored by the provisions of the settlement.

Fitzwilliam chuckled under his breath. Miss Carteret's bright, glittering eyes revealed a woman of very great intelligence and a very strong will, who appreciated the opportunity to test her influence on the man who wished to be her husband.

He was as malleable in her hands as Elizabeth suggested he had been in her mother's hands. Luckily, Miss Carteret seemed a kind and sensible woman, the kind that would help restore his affairs and steer him to a respectable future.

She was more than he deserved, but if she wanted a ductile man, then she would likely be satisfied with the match as well.

The baronet's settlement offer made, the Earl had to be approached. As predicted, Father was put out that his youngest son would arrange a marriage on his own. Darcy helped remind him that Miss Elliot was exactly the kind of match the Earl would have arranged had he been given the opportunity.

The logic of the argument and a decanter of excellent brandy eventually swayed him to accept the match and offer a generous settlement on the new couple. In truth, it was more than Fitzwilliam had expected, enough to free his conscience over the wedding gift he had indulged in for Elizabeth.

One more trip, back to the baronet for final signatures, and the business was complete. At last, Fitzwilliam and Darcy set off for Hartfield and to the women who waited for them.

No wonder Darcy loathed being away from Pemberley without Liza. It had not made sense before, but now, it seemed a very sensible thing indeed.

Elizabeth fell into the nearest parlor chair, the last rays of sunset fading into night. No doubt her posture was frightful, but Hartfield's parlor was comfortable and who would care when they were all so bone weary? Nearby, Mrs. Darcy and Mrs. Knightley—Liza and Emma they were to her now—did the same. Listingbrook Manor was by no means frightfully unkempt, but without a family in residence, or anyone to guide the minimal staff properly, it was in great need of attention. So it fell on her to make it ready for them to take residence.

Emma had brought two of her maids and a groundskeeper to assist their efforts. With them and the housekeeper and maid at Listingbrook, all three ladies, donned aprons and pushed up their sleeves for a solid ten days of grueling labor.

Everything in the closets, drawers, and chests smelt musty. It must have been put away still damp at some point, a common enough error for an inattentive maid to make. But oh, the work it left now! All the linens from every room had to be washed. At least the housekeeper found it as shocking as Elizabeth did.

The maids handled the laundry. Hauling the wood and water, soaking it in lye, boiling it and agitating it. Rinsing and wringing, then spreading it over the drying grounds. Elizabeth divided her time between supervising the maids and assisting the ladies who were sweeping and scrubbing the interior.

How was it possible for so much dust to accumulate? All but the master's bedroom and study seemed covered in layers of it. How had she missed that on her first visit to the house?

She pressed a groom and Emma's groundskeeper into service beating carpets, moving furniture, and hauling firewood. Thank heavens the house was not any larger, or they might never have finished before the men returned.

But they had. According to Fitzwilliam's letter, they would return tomorrow, after having settled all matters with both families. Hopefully he would be pleased with their efforts. At least he could be assured of her diligence in managing household affairs in his absence. That should be something.

The housekeeper brought a tray of hot cider and biscuits. She wrapped stiff fingers around the mug and breathed in the warm, sweet vapors. Delightful, simply delightful.

Liza did the same. She caught Elizabeth's eye and they giggled, too weary to be proper and too companionable to care. How good it was to have women to call friends—real friends.

"Ah, that is a sound I have longed to hear." Mr. Darcy, still in his greatcoat, stood in the doorway.

"See what I have found on our doorstep!" Mr. Knightley chuckled, ushering Mr. Darcy and Fitzwilliam into the parlor.

A moment later, Liza was beside Mr. Darcy, hidden in his embrace.

"I am pleased to see you, too." Fitzwilliam leaned close.

When had she gone to his side?

"Damn it all, it has been too long." He wrapped his arms around her and pulled her close.

His coat still bore traces of the cool night air, but she nestled into his chest.

No wonder Anne did not spurn Wentworth's improper displays. How absolutely satisfying this was.

The gentlemen's valets trundled in to relieve them of their coats, and the housekeeper brought more cider and sandwiches.

"To what do we own this lovely surprise? Your letter said that you would arrive tomorrow," Mrs. Darcy said.

"I told you they would be early, did I not?" Knightley winked and waved them to sit.

"A man intent on getting married is difficult to gainsay." Darcy sat beside Liza, cradling a mug of cider.

"I admit it is true, but I will not apologize." Fitzwilliam stared into Elizabeth's eyes.

His eyes were the most unique shade of gray-blue—so unusual, so compelling. She could stare into them for hours.

Dear, dear man.

"So, your errands, they went well?" Emma bit her lower lip, her voice very soft.

Fitzwilliam leaned back, crossing one leg over the other. "Indeed. Though I confess, I tend to distrust things that are so easy."

"Easy? You call that easy? That is certainly not what you were claiming at Matlock House in London." Darcy rolled his eyes and took a deep draw off his cider. "I seem to recall a conversation with a father that lasted well into sunrise."

"Compared to what I expected, it was quite easy." Fitzwilliam laced his fingers and stretched until his knuckles popped.

"Were there objections from your family?" Elizabeth whispered.

"No, I would hardly call them objections." Fitzwilliam caught her gaze again.

The tightness in her chest eased.

"Then what would you call that shouting, stomping display from your father?" Darcy reached for a sandwich.

Emma gasped, wide-eyed, and covered her mouth.

"Father displaying his plumage." Fitzwilliam shrugged and winked at Elizabeth. "He is rather like a gamebird, making certain everyone sees and understands his rank. It was nothing. His temper is a very different thing. Perhaps you did not notice, but there was nary an oath involved. Until he breaks out the epithets, there is no temper involved at all."

Elizabeth snickered. No wonder he knew how to deal with her father.

"I wondered where you got that habit from." Darcy's eyebrows flashed.

"So then, the earl was in agreement?" Emma asked.

"He was delighted to dispose of me to a suitable woman." Fitzwilliam laced his hands behind his head.

"Suitable?" Elizabeth held her breath.

"Absolutely. My mother and sisters voiced no objections, either. Having met you in Bath, they found your manners quite charming."

Her cheeks heated—but how could they not, the way he stared at her. "And my father?"

Fitzwilliam snorted softly. "He tried to fluff his feathers as well."

"But was quite checked by the object of his ..." Darcy's voice trailed off and he looked to Liza.

"Affections?" Liza cocked her head.

"Interests?" Knightley leaned forward.

Darcy pointed at him. "That is more accurate."

"Miss Carteret was supportive?" Elizabeth's jaw dropped.

"Suspiciously so." Darcy flashed a quick glance at Liza who chewed her lower lip and nodded.

"I expect happy news will be arriving from him fairly soon. He seemed to be ready to press his solicitor into service as soon as our marriage articles were signed, and expressed interest in purchasing an ordinary license."

So Father was getting his wish—a young wife who might bear him a son and cut off the heir presumptive from his line.

"Do you think it will be a happy match?" Emma glanced at Knightley.

Fitzwilliam shrugged. "I cannot predict a man's happiness, but she seems to be well aware of the situation and content with it. Though I did not know the first Lady Elliot, I believe that Miss Carteret has some strong similarities to her."

Elizabeth nodded. That would be good for both of them then. For all his peculiarities, Father did not deserve to be unhappy.

"So then, we are free to make plans for a wedding?" The words barely escaped her tight throat.

Fitzwilliam turned that gaze on her again. "What say you? Are you ready?"

"The papers are in order, the house is in order—so yes, I believe a wedding is in order."

He took her hand and kissed it.

Blood rushed to her face, and the room spun a little.

Mr. Knightley rose. "Come, Darcy, let us break the news to my father and Bennet. I doubt they will find it nearly as exciting as our ladies—they do so love the disruptions that such celebrations bring."

"Perhaps not, but they will enjoy the wedding breakfast well enough." Emma laughed as they left.

Liza and Emma huddled together.

Fitzwilliam rose and urged her to follow him to the far corner of the room, as if to show her a book from the shelves there.

How sweet of Liza to turn her back to them.

"The house is prepared? Is that what I have to thank for the adorable smudge on your cheek?" He traced the crest of her cheek with his thumb.

She closed her eyes and sighed. Yes, his fingers were hard and calloused, but no touch could be more welcome.

"You do not think we sat about painting screens and netting purses whilst you were away?"

"No, I did not. It looks like all of you—"

"And a number of Emma's staff—"

"Emma?"

Elizabeth nodded.

"I am very glad you have a friend so close now."

"I am more glad to have you so close right now."

"Miss Elliot! I am shocked!" That is not what his eyes said.

"I would be shocked if you did not return the sentiment." She ran her tongue over her lips.

"I cannot have that, can I?"

Oh, his smile! How could such a simple expression send warmth all the way down to her toes? But it did.

His eyebrows twitched as he winked and leaned in very close.

His lips were still a mite cold, but that did not last long as the heat between them built.

Is this what Liza and Emma had hinted at as they suggested that separate chambers for master and mistress might not be the only choice in room arrangements?

Strong and hard, his hands pressed against her back, drawing her as close as they could possibly be. Her breath hitched.

Oh!

Behind them, Liza coughed just loudly enough.

Fitzwilliam grumbled under his breath and slowly released her, but the longing in his eyes—he was no happier than she was about it.

"Soon—as soon as can be arranged," she whispered in his ear.

"Saturday?"

"Three days seems sufficient—even generous, Fitzwilliam." She feathered her lips over his ear as she dragged out every syllable of his name.

"Elizabeth!" He nibbled just below her jaw near her ear.

Oh!

Perhaps Friday might be possible.

Saturday morning—Friday was unfortunately too soon for the butcher to prepare Emma's order—Elizabeth stood before the mirror in her second-best gown. No, it was not new, but it was silk, and pale blue, and lovely. Perhaps she ought to be wearing her best gown, but Fitzwilliam's favorite color was blue, and somehow pleasing him seemed more important than wearing a slightly-newer gown.

Father, with Miss Carteret and the Dowager Lady Dalrymple, waited downstairs. Miss Carteret, who seemed disposed to be sentimental, insisted that Father should present the bride to her groom. They would be attending the wedding breakfast, too, gracing Hartfield with their presence and titles, thus lifting the status of her wedding out of the mundane.

Such a thoughtful gift, albeit a cheap one, considering what the earl had settled upon them.

That was an ungracious thought, especially after the settlement Father had agreed to—with the encouragement of Miss Carteret. It was equal to, if not slightly more generous than, the settlements to Mary and Anne.

Had she not been so fond of Fitzwilliam, it would have been important, but now it was just merely trivia.

The truly important thing was that Fitzwilliam would be waiting for her at the church and in just an hour, perhaps a wee bit more, he would be her husband.

"Are you ready?" Liza peeked in.

"I think so. What do you think?"

"You are everything a bride should be, my dear. Have you thought of any further questions?" Liza took her hand with all the tenderness of a sister.

Her cheeks heated. "I think not. Our conversation yesterday was quite … thorough."

Liza bit her lower lip. "I believe I warned you once that directness was my way, uncomfortable though it may be at times."

"I do appreciate it, and I think he will as well." She looked away, anything not to meet Liza's inquiring gaze.

"That was the point of the exercise. My sister Mary was equally mortified when I sat with her before her wedding, but later she told me she was glad for it. Shall we go now?"

Hopefully, Fitzwilliam would be, too.

Elizabeth picked up her cloak and muff and followed Liza downstairs.

Father escorted Miss Carteret and Lady Dalrymple in their coach, leaving the ladies to go in Knightley's carriage. The men followed on horseback.

Emma and Liza exchanged encouraging glances with her, but they had little to say. Probably for the best. She was too nervous for conversation.

Though not asked, it seemed Mrs. Elton had seen to the decoration of the church. No doubt the gesture was more to insert herself into the proceedings and claim credit for their success than out of any fondness for Elizabeth. Still though, it was pleasant to see the church porch strewn with rushes and flowers, and the inside of the chapel appointed with several attractive bouquets, offering a welcoming perfume as they entered.

Father escorted his ladies to their seats and joined her at the back of the church. Mr. Elton approached them, fawning. Elizabeth stepped back and allowed Father to enjoy the attention without her.

Long, heavy steps approached and stopped just behind her. A shadow leaned close and whispered in her ear, "Despite knowing Darcy was escorting you, it is still a relief to see you here."

His voice sent delightful little shivers down the back of her neck. "I am pleased to see you here as well." She clasped her hands behind her back.

He covered both her hands with his large, calloused one, barely lacing fingers with her.

She must not smile—not too much—and give their secret away. What a thrill to be so bold and improper with so many witnesses.

A quick glance over her shoulder revealed the same thought written in his twinkling eyes set above a very square and proper jaw.

They must invite Anne and Wentworth to stay soon. The two men were so similar. They would relish each other's company.

He squeezed her hand and sauntered to the front of the church. His long, easy steps betrayed his mood—his steps always did.

Mr. Elton called them to order, and Father paraded her to the front, making a very great show of presenting her to Fitzwilliam for the reading of the service. It seemed only a moment later Fitzwilliam slipped a braided gold band over her finger, and she presented him with a sturdy, plain one. Mr. Elton trundled them to the back of the church for the signing of the marriage lines.

And it was done. She was now a married woman.

"Come, Mrs. Fitzwilliam." He placed her hand in the crook of his arm.

He had that look in his eye. Mischievous. Pleased with himself. Playful. The one she anticipated and—if she were honest—adored.

"Close your eyes and walk with me."

Did he not realize that it was nearly impossible to think, much less obey, when he whispered in her ear like that? And completely impossible when he brushed the side of her neck with his lips.

"Do you not trust me, my dear?"

"Teasing man! Just remember you are not the only one who can play at such things."

"I count on it. Now, step over the threshold and outside. Just a few more steps. Now open your eyes."

A freshly-painted carriage waited before her. A matching pair of bay horses regarded her placidly.

"Later today we will go riding, but I thought perhaps you might like to ride to your wedding breakfast in your own carriage. I confess it is not new. It has enjoyed years of service to Listingbrook. But I have had it refitted for the occasion." He opened the door for her.

"A carriage?" Her vision blurred, and her eyes burned. A new carriage had been out of the question—she had not even brought up the notion. But this—such a perfect gift.

"Of course, Mrs. Fitzwilliam—"

Oh, the way he said that!

"How else will you make your bridal visits around the neighborhood?" He handed her into the carriage.

Buttery soft leather seats invited her into the warm interior, heated by wrapped bricks. Fresh, crisp white curtains covered the side glass, letting in just enough light to enjoy the expression on his face.

He was so pleased with himself.

He deserved to be.

"I am perfectly delighted with it—with you and with everything." She slipped across the carriage to sit beside him and settled in very close.

He slid his arm around her shoulder and pressed a kiss to the top of her head. Tension drained from him, and he leaned into her, warm and heavy. "Mrs. Fitzwilliam, you have made me a very happy man."

"Then you, sir, are far too easy to please."

"Let us hope you continue thinking so for quite a long time." He tipped her chin up and pressed his lips to hers.

Yes, let it be a very long time indeed.

✣ Author's Note

Ape Leaders and Vermin of the State: The Unmarried of the Regency Era

REGENCY SOCIETY ORGANIZED itself around marriage and family. Adults were identified by their place, or lack thereof, in a married, family unit. Married women were ranked higher and more respected than the unmarried. Married men were perceived as having come into their own and given the esteem and authority that went with such an accomplishment.

The plight of the regency spinster is fairly well understood. The local tax or judicial records says it all. Women were typically identified in tax or judicial records by their marital status (spinsters, wives and widows) whereas men were always identified by their occupation or social status. (Shoemaker, 1998) A woman's identity (and legal existence) was determined by her marital status.

Spinsterhood was considered 'unnatural' for a woman, even though nearly one in four upper class girls remained unmarried (Day, 2006). They were called 'ape-leaders' (for that was what they would be doing in hell as punishment for the unnatural lifestyle. Enough said on that point….) and ridiculed for their failure in the most basic requirements of femininity.

However, if a single woman possessed independent means—a fortune of her own sufficient for her to live on, it was possible she could maintain her own household and carry on an independent life. Female investors were not unknown and their capital supported the joint stock companies behind municipal utilities and railways. Wise investments could provide a steady income without administrative worries. (Davidoff & Hall, 2002)

Not all women were so fortunate as to have independent means, and even if they were, male relatives might make it difficult or impossible for her to access her own fortune. (Naturally the men in her life knew better how to manage her affairs than she.) In those cases, a spinster would have two choices, find a job to support herself or live in the house of a relative.

Upper class ladies had limited job prospects, given their desire to remain respectable—and their more or less complete lack of marketable skills. Genteel options were limited to being a lady's companion or a governess.

Being a governess required and education that not all ladies had and was not necessarily an enviable position. Within the households they served, the existed in a nether realm, not equal to the family but above the servants. Often, a governess would associate with neither, virtually shut away from all society. She would also be vulnerable, as all female servants were, to (unwanted) advances from the males of the house-hold.

Unmarried women unable to become governesses were expected to make themselves useful to which ever relative might take them in. They might keep house for bachelor (or widowed) brothers or uncles, tend children, cover for married sisters while they were indisposed or during lying-in, nurse the sick, cook, clean and mend. Ironically, despite these functions, they were still often considered spungers and a burden to the household.

Today, most believe that bachelors of the era enjoyed the same social position as married men, free from the prejudice spinsters experienced. However, they too were touched by the societal bias toward the married.

This is not to say, though, that they were in any way as put upon as spinsters. The scarcity value of men in the era gave eligible bachelors the power to act as connoisseurs, holding off until the 'right' situation came along. (Jones, 2009) For younger sons of gentlemen, whom primogeniture denied substantial inheritance, marriage was likely to make him significantly less well off, unless of course he could find himself an heiress or woman with an excellent dowry. So, these men typically waited for marriage, often until their early thirties. But this time, they would have worked long enough to have established themselves in their profession and have the means to support a family (or attract a woman with money, which would always be an attractive alternative.)

Nonetheless, like upper-class women, one out of four younger sons remained lifelong bachelors

(Jones, 2009) While bachelorhood was seen as a natural (and possibly necessary for wealth-gathering) phase of life, the lifelong bachelor was a different creature altogether. Though not subject to the vicious ridicule heaped on spinsters, bachelors were subject to degradation as well.

In marriage, a young man took up the burdens (and the dividends—don't forget those) of patriarchy, and became a fully realized man. In a very real sense, a man achieved political adulthood when he could support his dependents and represent their interests in the public forum. Failure to marry was often seen as being unrealized in masculinity, at the mercy of impulses and negligent in the duties to society.

"Perpetual bachelors were the 'vermin of the state' pronounced *The Women's Advocate* … 'They enjoy the benefits of Society, but Contribute not to its Charge and spunge upon the publick, without making the least return.'" (Vickery, 2009) The strength of this sentiment led to punitive taxes being placed upon bachelor households.

In 1785, employers of one or two male servants paid an annual £1, 5 shillings for each of them. All bachelors over 21 (the ae of majority) had to pay an extra £1, 5 shillings for every male servant they employed. Female servants were taxed at a lower rate, but bachelors had to pay double the amount. (Horn, 2004) And of course, as taxes go, the rates only increased as time went on.

Unless they were able to set up housekeeping with an unmarried female relation, sister, niece, aunt, etc. (Not a cousin mind you as they were considered marriageable and living with them unmarried would have been unacceptable.) a bachelor would have also had to pay for services usually rendered by female labor. The top four occupations for women in London 1200-1850 were washing, charring (cleaning) nursing and the making/mending of clothes, reflecting the needs of bachelors. Few women noted prostitution as their occupation, but that was a thriving trade as well. So, not did bachelors pay for their choice not to settle down and make legitimate babies in loss of social status, and taxes, but basic domestic comforts cost them dearly as well.

So, unmarried men may not have been leading apes in hell, according to regency standards, but being considered selfish social vermin was hardly desirable either. The attitude was hardly surprising though when the fundamental unit of society was the male-headed, conjugal household.

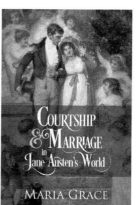

If you enjoyed this tidbit, you might want to check out: ***Courtship and Marriage in Jane Austen's World,*** available at your favorite online booksellers.

References

Baird, Rosemary. *Mistress of the House: Great Ladies and Grand Houses, 1670-1830.* London: Phoenix, 2004.

Collins, Irene. *Jane Austen, the Parson's Daughter.* London: Hambledon Press, 1998.

Davidoff, Leonore, and Catherine Hall. *Family Fortunes: Men and Women of the English Middle Class, 1780-1850.* Chicago: University of Chicago Press, 1987.

Day, Malcom. *Voices from the World of Jane Austen.*

David&Charles, 2006.

Jones, Hazel. *Jane Austen and Marriage*. London: Continuum, 2009.

Horn, Pamela. *Flunkeys and scullions: life below stairs in Georgian England*. Stroud: Sutton, 2004.

Laudermilk, Sharon H., and Teresa L. Hamlin. *The Regency Companion*. New York: Garland, 1989.

Martin, Joanna. *Wives and Daughters: Women and Children in the Georgian Country House*. London: Hambledon and London, 2004.

Shoemaker, Robert Brink. *Gender in English Society, 1650-1850: The Emergence of Separate Spheres?* London: Longman, 1998. Pearson Education Limited

The Woman's advocate or The baudy batchelor out in his calculation: Being the genuine answer paragraph by paragraph, to the batchelor's estimate plainly proving that marriage is to a man of sense and oeconomy, both a happiner and less chargeablo state, than a single life. Written for the honour of the good wives, and pretty girls of old England. London: Printed for A. Moore, near St. Paul's, 1729.

Vickery, Amanda. *Behind Closed Doors: At Home in Georgian England*. New Haven, Conn.: Yale University Press, 2009.

Vickery, Amanda. *The Gentleman's Daughter: Women's Lives in Georgian England*. New Haven, Conn.: Yale University Press, 1998.

❧Acknowledgments

SO MANY PEOPLE have helped me along the journey taking this from an idea to a reality.

Julie, Anji, Debbie, Ruth and Susanne thank you so much for cold reading, proof reading and being honest!

And my dear friend Cathy, my biggest cheerleader, you have kept me from chickening out more than once!

And my sweet sister Gerri who believed in even those first attempts that now live in the file drawer!

Thank you!

✤Other Books by Maria Grace

Remember the Past
The Darcy Brothers

Given Good Principles Series:

Darcy's Decision
The Future Mrs. Darcy
All the Appearance of Goodness
Twelfth Night at Longbourn

Jane Austen's Dragons Series:

Pemberley: Mr. Darcy's Dragon

The Queen of Rosings Park Series:

Mistaking Her Character
The Trouble to Check Her

Sweet Tea Stories:

A Spot of Sweet Tea: Hopes and Beginnings (short
story anthology)
The Darcy's First Christmas
Snowbound at Hartfield

Regency Life (Nonfiction) Series:

A Jane Austen Christmas: Regency Christmas Tradi-
tions
Courtship and Marriage in Jane Austen's World

Short Stories:

Four Days in April
Sweet Ginger
Last Dance
Not Romantic
To Forget

Available in paperback, e-book, and audiobook format at all online bookstores.

On Line Exclusives at:

www.http//RandomBitsofFascination.com

Bonus and deleted scenes
Regency Life Series

Free e-books:
Bits of Bobbin Lace
The Scenes Jane Austen Never Wrote: First Anniversaries
Half Agony, Half Hope: New Reflections on Persuasion
Four Days in April
Jane Bennet in January
February Aniversaries

About the Author

Though Maria Grace has been writing fiction since she was ten years old, those early efforts happily reside in a file drawer and are unlikely to see the light of day again, for which many are grateful. After penning five file-drawer novels in high school, she took a break from writing to pursue college and earn her doctorate in Educational Psychology. After 16 years of university teaching, she returned to her first love, fiction writing.

She has one husband and one grandson, two graduate degrees and two black belts, three sons, four undergraduate majors, five nieces, is starting her sixth year blogging on Random Bits of Fascination, has built seven websites, attended eight English country dance balls, sewn nine Regency era costumes, and shared her life with ten cats.

She can be contacted at:

author.MariaGrace@gmail.com

Facebook:
http://facebook.com/AuthorMariaGrace

On Amazon.com:
http://amazon.com/author/mariagrace

Random Bits of Fascination
(http://RandomBitsofFascination.com)

Austen Variations (http://AustenVariations.com)

English Historical Fiction Authors
(http://EnglshHistoryAuthors.blogspot.com)

White Soup Press (http://whitesouppress.com/)

On Twitter @WriteMariaGrace

On Pinterest: http://pinterest.com/mariagrace423/